GW00647278

CRIME FICTION

CRIME FICTION

UEA MA
Creative Writing Anthologies
2019

CONTENTS

MICK HERRON
Foreword

Some while ago I met a man who told me he'd once tried writing a novel. His problem, he explained, was that he'd only really wanted to write 'the good bits', as he called them. Having completed these he lost interest, and all he was left with was a patchwork of unconnected scenes.

He had fallen, of course, into a common error: that of believing that a novel has good bits. Or, put another way, he'd failed to appreciate the novelist's fundamental task, which is to feel that he or she is always working on the good bits. Open any Dickens novel at random and you'll find him in full flow; pick any paragraph by Jane Austen, there'll be a line worth reading aloud. Neither saved their energy for the story's highlights. They left it all on the page, every time.

Judging by the extracts contained in this anthology, those undertaking the University of East Anglia's MA in Crime Fiction have had this lesson drummed into them. Against settings ranging from London in the '60s, through Norwich past and present, to an independent Scotland in the near future, and whether writing about snow in Tokyo or big-game poaching in Kenya, about artists, private eyes or music-hall artistes, they've left it all on the page. In doing so, their only point in common is that each has chosen to work within the crime genre. This in itself is neither surprising – it's abundantly clear that the genre offers scope for both escaping from the anxieties generated by a body politic in disarray, and for examining those anxieties and their causes – nor is it especially significant. Genre is frequently thought of as being a series of border walls, when in reality it amounts to little more than road markings. Crime, romance, fantasy, even actual "literature": what novels in these different lanes share is that they are novels; that this is the vehicle their author has chosen. But then, the purpose of writing a novel is not having a particular journey in mind, or even a particular story to tell. It's having the need to write.

It's not only the writer who has work to do, of course. Readers have their part to play too, and it seems only fair that they should be held to the same high standards that they expect writers to meet, ideally matching those reached by Sloppy in *Our Mutual Friend*, of whom it is famously observed, 'You mightn't think it, but Sloppy is a beautiful reader ... He do the Police in different voices'. Doing the Police in different voices is the reader's job, but the writer's is to make that possible by treating everyone on the page – police and villain alike – with equal care, and by approaching every character's appearance as one of the good bits. The writers collected in this anthology have made that effort. Readers can happily rehearse their different voices, and look forward to being put to the test by the variety of opportunities on display here, in what is at once a snapshot of what the crime novel is doing now and a glimpse of the directions it might take in the future. It's a comfort to know that this part of the future, at least, is in steady hands.

HENRY SUTTON
Introduction

Parameters, or borders if you like, are there to be crossed, dismantled, traversed. Writing of note and innovation inhabits edgelands – places of undefined territory. Genre fiction no more so. We at UEA champion the dynamism of good writing, the breaking of literary rules, the freedom of movement. Over the next one hundred and twenty pages or so, you will encounter extraordinary space, shaped by writers willing to be a part of a bigger project. You could call that project progression, or a partnership, or indeed a community. And that's the thing about creative writing, as in all writing. It is a collaboration and a pact. Writers are readers and readers are writers, of course, each leading the other through new fields of discovery. I'd like to thank all the writers here for also being such committed and insightful readers. Everyone has played a part in what follows.

The creative writing workshop is an environment that is built upon freedom, but also support. It's almost too magical a place, too idyllic, too democratic, too truthful. But I don't believe in magic, any more than I believe in the muse. What has happened in this space, which is ever expanding, over the last couple of years, has been an outpouring of talent and determination, by eleven extraordinary writers. It's been a joy observing such work, such results, while also knowing that the pleasure will continue as each writer here develops further and finds new audiences, new paths, new borders to be crossed and dismantled. Of course, not everyone can be so supportive, and some borders, some views, will always remain a little stubborn and outdated. However, I like to think that the crime writing and reading public is an especially broad and accommodating community, built on those guiding principles of freedom, of inclusivity.

It's also a fun community, despite some of the darker themes and more difficult issues that are encountered and explored. Indeed, it is just this scope that makes the form, the space, so enduring, dynamic and accepting. The reality is we're happy to engage with hard crime fiction as readily as soft crime fiction, as long as it's beautifully, and innovatively, written. The following extracts attest to this.

This diverse anthology comprises the latest work from the 2019 cohort of crime fiction writers studying UEA's renowned Creative Writing MA.

Laura Ashton's research into the career of her grandfather, Mr Justice Melford Stevenson, led her to apply for the Crime Fiction MA. Laura's fiction explores the circumstances that led to the trials, with a focus on understanding criminal behaviour and interrogating legal injustices. She has an MA in Women, Gender and Writing and has worked on high profile feminist campaigns.

Twitter: @ashtonlaura
Instagram: @lauraashton
l.ashtonhill@gmail.com

This Is What Will Happen

The body lies, almost entirely, in the back room of the shop. Only the feet stray beyond the boundary of the space that is marked off by a sign that reads: 'PRIVATE.' Beneath a flimsy curtain, hanging from a bent rail, the soles of well-worn court shoes are all that would be seen by anyone who came through the door.

Behind the curtain, the room is small and narrow. She lies amongst chair legs, pokers for a coal fire, jugs and scraps of string. It is March and the shop is cold. She wears two cardigans; one buttoned up; another open.

Her hands curl softly across her body in what could have been their natural sleeping position every night of the 59 years she lived. An unusual sculptural ring embraces her wedding finger, it is out of keeping with her demure dress. On her beige cardigan, her left hand rests below the dagger that protrudes out of her chest. The blade is nine inches long and has pierced her heart. The ivory handle has had its price tag ripped off and lies astray; drowned in blood. Her fingers aren't reaching for the dagger, it's as if they know they are helpless in the prevention of this attack. Her face tells a different story.

Rigid in shock, or is it anger? Her eyes stare up as large as half-crown coins. Her short grey hair flops backwards and mixes with the congealed blood that has permeated into the wooden floor beneath. Her mouth gapes open, in a shape that could have formed a gasp; a scream; or an enraged expression of expletives. Her skin is as pale as the whites of her eyes that encircle her black pupils. More blood is smeared from the side of her mouth all the way to her right ear and there is a dent in her head. A stone ornament lies nearby on its side.

To her left, a brass statuette faces an electric fire that isn't on. A large fawn-coloured handbag sits on an armchair close by. It is unzipped and open. Inside, amongst letters and keys, remains her purse. The shop's till contains all its money. The curios and artefacts, that the shop is crammed with, are undisturbed. Only one item appears to be missing. An Indian ornamental dress sword no longer hangs from its hook and a single sheet of brown wrapping paper has been removed from the pile.

It was morning and a thick fog hung in the air as Alfie hurried along Cecil Court. The street lamps that lined the central path were still lit, glowing yellow through the grey haze. Alfie's black mac flapped behind him, the buttons undone as the coat didn't reach around the package he was attempting to conceal beneath.

In his haste, he tripped on a cobblestone and nearly fell, but caught himself just in time. The package slipped and he fumbled with hands clad in thick gloves. He looked around, his eyes flitting between the shop windows as the workers inside prepared for the day ahead. On his left, a hairdresser stirred something in a bowl. She lifted a gloopy spoon and watched the substance drop down. Opposite, a bookseller opened envelopes with a letter opener, his head lowered, reading the contents. Alfie kept going.

As he neared the end of the street, a man in a bowler hat turned the corner and Alfie moved closer to the wall, hunching up his shoulders as he tried to hide his face inside the upturned collar of his raincoat. He held the package tightly and could feel his heart beating behind it. Alfie looked over his shoulder and saw the man had moved on without so much as a glance in his direction. Alfie turned the corner onto St Martin's Lane.

To his left he could make out the shop he wanted. But it wouldn't be open yet. He crossed the road and turned right. A Lyons van was parked outside the teashop where his sister worked. He longed to go and see Lillian, but the package digging into his ribs reminded him she was better off out of it. Instead, he took a turning to his left. A path so narrow it was as though someone had come along with a large knife and sliced a slit between the adjacent buildings. He squeezed through and hurried along the passage.

It was a good place to wait, with three possible escape routes if required. He could turn back the way he came, continue on, or there was another option; midway along there was a tunnel under the buildings. He glanced down it as he passed. There was movement under a pile of boxes and Alfie took a step back. A stray cat appeared from underneath, its green eyes, piercingly bright, followed him as he walked on.

At the far end the wall jutted out, creating a corner, perfect for hiding behind. He leaned against it, listening to his heartbeat and watching his breath disappear into the fog.

Something brushed against his foot and he jumped. A small rat was sniffing his shoe. He kicked out and it ran away. The tip of its string-like tail was the last of it to be swallowed up by the fog. A high-pitched squealing sound confirmed the rat had chosen the wrong path. Alfie looked down at his shoe, he dug the toe end into the dirt.

In the distance he heard a siren. He huddled further into the corner, trying to ignore the whiffs of urine. His hands were sweating inside the gloves as he clutched hold of the package. To distract himself, he stared at the wall ahead and imagined Lillian on the other side. She would be bustling about in the black and white uniform, with cups of coffee and cooked breakfasts. If he was there, she'd be refilling his tea and sneaking him biscuits. He shifted uncomfortably against the rough wall.

A change in the light caused him to stiffen. For a moment the alleyway darkened. Alfie sensed a shadow passing in front of the electric wall light in the tunnel. He held his breath as a large shape appeared. Alfie lifted up his shoulders and pressed his face into the corner, hoping to be hidden by the fog. But it was too late, the man had seen him. When he spoke, his voice was loud and slurred, 'Hello, there.'

Quietly Alfie replied, 'Hello.'

He moved towards Alfie, swaying slightly. A vile stench wafted with him and the skin on his cheeks was weathered red.

'Got any smokes?'

Alfie shook his head.

'Whatcha got?' He pointed at the package.

Alfie gripped tighter. 'Nothing.'

The man clapped his hands together. 'How d'you know?'

'Know what?'

'It's my birthday.' The man laughed loudly.

Alfie looked beyond him towards the entrance to the passage. 'Be quiet would you?'

'Only if you tell me what's in it?'

'Then will you go away?'

'Per'aps.'

'Present for my girl.'

'You got a sweetheart?'

Alfie nodded.

'What she look like?'

The corners of Alfie's lips twitched almost to a smile and, although his instincts were telling him to keep the conversation short, he couldn't resist answering the question. 'She's beautiful. Golden hair, dazzling blue eyes.'

'Blonde you say?' The man peered closely at Alfie with a quizzical expression.

Alfie bit his lip.

The man shrugged. 'Why not? I had a sweetheart once. Betty. Brunette. Curves everywhere.' His hands moved around in the air as though groping Betty's invisible body. 'I bloody loved her. Suppose you want to know what 'appened?'

Alfie didn't say anything, but he maintained eye contact.

The man leaned closer and spoke quietly. 'I did something bad. Very bad,' he shook his head. Alfie thought he saw tears in his eyes, but it could have been the fog. 'She found out and left me.'

Alfie regretted showing any interest as the man's voice rose again and he started calling, 'Oh Betty, where are you? Betty!'

Alfie spoke firmly, 'Go away would you?'

The man stopped wailing. 'No. You ain't told me what you got in your wrapper?'

Alfie looking down. 'It's an umbrella.'

'An umbrella,' he repeated, rolling his r's as he said it again, 'An umbrrrrrrella.' Then he laughed. 'That's not a very good present.'

Alfie mumbled, 'She needs one.'

'You'll have to do better than that if you want to keep blondie.'

He looked past him, there was a gap in the fog, and he saw a tip of a top hat floating across the opening at the far end of the passage. 'Look, I told you. Now get lost.'

There was a moment's silence as the two men stared at each other. Their heads close enough for the hot air from their breath to meet in-between. Alfie smelt his breath. He winced. The man swiped a hand out and made a grab for the parcel. It was a quick, sudden movement from someone used to taking his chances. But Alfie reacted faster. He pushed him and the man stumbled backwards; hitting his back against the wall. He groaned and rubbed his chest where Alfie had pushed him.

'Whatcha do that for? I only wanted a look ...'

Alfie stuck out his thumb and jerked it in the direction of the tunnel. 'Piss off.'

The man snorted, picked himself up and hobbled away. As he disappeared down the tunnel Alfie heard him say, 'Umbrella, my arse.'

Alfie looked behind him. He didn't have a watch, but he guessed enough time had passed. He slid out from behind the wall and turned left onto the street at the back. The mist was lifting, and the package was large and cumbersome in his hands.

Back on St Martin's Lane he watched two men in overalls cross the road holding tins of paint. A woman was leaning out of the upstairs window of a pub.

'Watch out below,' she shouted as she tipped over an ashtray. Alfie dodged out the way of falling cigarette butts. He caught sight of one half smoked and stooped to pick it up, before hurrying down the street. He came to a standstill when he reached the shop. He'd never been in a gunsmith's before and took a moment to gather himself. Placing his hand on the polished doorknob, he took a deep breath before going inside.

He was surprised to note the cluster of acne spots on the forehead of the man standing behind the counter. He wore a black suit that hung loosely around his torso, as though he'd recently had a growth spurt and the rest of his body hadn't filled out yet. Alfie breathed out. The man couldn't have been more than sixteen and, being four years older, Alfie was glad of the advantage.

The young man put away the cloth he was holding. 'Good morning, how can I help you?'

'Morning,' said Alfie and moved over to the counter. It doubled as a display cabinet and underneath were an array of different size guns, glass oil bottles and cartridges. He placed the package on top. 'I have this to sell.' He pushed it over and gestured for the man to open it. But he didn't move.

'I'm afraid you've come at a bad time.'

'You'll want to see this,' said Alfie.

The young man glanced down as Alfie peeled back the paper. 'It's very nice ...'

'Nice? It's quality. Look at the handle.'

'But I'm afraid I don't have the authority to buy anything without my father's permission.'

'What's your name?' Asked Alfie.

'George.'

'Listen, George. I paid thirty quid for it. But I'm only going to ask for fifteen.'

'Even so, I'm afraid I can't ...'

'Fifteen pounds! Half of what it's worth!'

'You'll need to speak to my father.'

'Look,' said Alfie. 'I'm a bit tight for time.' He made a point of checking the wall clock. It was five past nine. 'How about I leave it with you?'

'Oh no, you can't do that. Not without it being prearranged.' George tore a piece of Scotch tape off a dispenser and used it to hold the paper in place, as though that closed the conversation.

Alfie began to jig his leg, he glanced at the window.

'What time's your dad back?'

'Should be here by midday. Why don't you come back then?'

Alfie walked over to the window. His gloves were still on his hands and he absent-mindedly ran a hand back over his hair, as though he wasn't wearing any. Outside he could make out the distinctive shape of a policeman walking along the other side of the road. The point of his helmet seemed to cut a pathway through the fog. Alfie moved away from the window and back to the counter.

'I've got to be somewhere in a few minutes. I can't take it with me. How about I leave it here and pop back in the afternoon – once your dad's had a chance to have a look at it?'

'I don't know,' George looked around. 'We're very tight for space ...'

Alfie raised his voice, 'If he ain't interested, I'll take it back.'

'It's not really something we ...'

'Let's see what your dad thinks, all right?' And with that he turned and left before George had a chance to say anything else.

—

Lillian felt the boy watching her as she poured his lemonade. She hurried over to him, thinking he must be thirsty. But when she handed him the glass, instead of saying thank you, he looked her in the eye and said, 'She's a Comanchero.'

Lillian frowned. She caught sight of her reflection in the wall mirror and, seeing some strands of black hair had escaped, tucked them back under her cap.

His mother laughed, 'He loves playing Cowboys and Indians.'

With some effort, Lillian put on a smile. 'I'll just fetch your cakes.'

Behind the counter she hovered, looking for the smallest cream slices she could find, but unfortunately Lyons were pretty consistent with their sizes. She chose two and walked back over.

'I'm gonna get you, Comanchero,' said the boy. He formed his hand into a gun shape and pointed it at Lillian. 'Take that. Pow. Pow.'

She looked at his mother to see if she was going to say anything, but her nose was buried in a copy of *Woman's Own*. Lillian lent closer to him. Without making a sound, her mouth formed the words, 'Shut up.' It was over in seconds, but it had the desired effect because the boy sat back and raised his eyebrows. Lillian stood and walked away, the corners of her mouth turning upwards.

'There's a pretty smile to brighten my day,' said one of the market traders.

'Morning Fred, what can I get you?' she asked, still smiling. With his broken nose and hefty frame, it was always a pleasing surprise that he carried the scent of roses with him.

'I've been dreaming of your eggs and bacon all morning,' said Fred, as he rubbed the belly that protruded over the top of his apron.

'Been busy this morning?' She slid the egg onto his plate.

'Nah, no one about. It's the bloody fog again. Who's gonna buy flowers when they can't even see 'em?'

Lillian laughed. 'Pack up early, did you?'

'Left the boy in charge while I get a quick breakfast in. Do us a sausage sarnie as well, would you? Said I'll bring one back for 'im.'

'Certainly,' she said, buttering the bread.

'Thought it were lifting there for a bit, but it's come down even heavier now.'

She handed him the sandwich bag. 'Hope it'll clear up for you.'

'Ta, love,' he took the bag and plate, and went off to find a seat.

A steady stream of customers kept her occupied for a while and it wasn't until it began to die down that she left the counter to tidy the tables. Working her way to the seat by the window, where the boy had sat, she stopped in her tracks. Cream and cake crumbs had been smeared on the glass in a shape that mildly resembled a cowboy hat.

'For gawd sake,' said Lillian. 'That little ...'

'What was that, Lillian?' It was Mrs Northcott's firm voice behind her.

'Nothing, Mrs Northcott,' she said.

'I'll be needing a word with ...' but her words were cut off as they both heard a crash in the shop downstairs. 'Stack the boxes neatly in the window – you'd think that wouldn't be too much to ask?' She bustled off leaving Lillian to wonder what she needed to speak to her about. Before she could get in any more trouble, she fetched a bowl of soapy water and began to wipe the cream off. As the glass became clearer, she saw that Fred had been right about the fog. She could hardly see along St Martin's Lane, and just as she was thinking this, she made out a hazy figure who reminded her of Alfie. He was walking close to the wall and quickly disappeared from sight. He'd been tall with dark hair, even wearing a black rain mac. But it couldn't have been Alfie; he'd be at work. She dropped the cloth back into the bowl and left the tearoom to empty it into the toilet upstairs. She moved slowly, careful not to splash water on the wallpaper. Just as she neared the top, she heard footsteps behind her and almost immediately a hand on her shoulder.

She froze for a moment before putting on an assertive voice, 'Who's that?'

'Shh, Lills, it's me.'

'Alfie?' She struggled to turn.

'Yeah.'

'Thought I saw you out the window. Why aren't you at work?'

'Doctor gave me a sick note.'

She looked down at him from her elevated step and thought his skin did look rather sallow. She wished the steps weren't so narrow so she could put the bowl down and feel his forehead to see if he was running a fever.

'You should be at home in bed.'

'I came to see you. Get out the house for a bit.' As he said this he turned away and looked down the stairs towards the window at the end of the landing. Lillian frowned.

'Something wrong, Alfie?'

He turned his head. 'What makes you say that?'

'I don't know, you seem a bit ... rattled?'

'Thing is, I found a package slung in a doorway ...' he looked behind again.

'Well?'

'It's at the gunsmith's.'

'You found a gun!'

'Reckon it's worth a packet. But the boy in the gunsmith's said he can't buy it without his dad's say so. I had to leave it there.'

She breathed out. 'Best place for it.'

'Just need to wait it out, 'til the old man gets back.'

'It might belong to one of them gangs. You don't want to get messed up with them.'

They stood in the narrow stairway, Alfie looking over his shoulder and Lillian looking down at his mass of thick black hair. At five foot three, she was used to craning her neck to look up at Alfie, it felt strange seeing him from this angle.

'Don't worry, sis.' He turned and smiled up at her. 'I'll be fine.' He pulled off his glove, reached out his hand and gave her arm a little squeeze. 'Just need to lie low for a bit.'

'What d'you need the money for anyway? Want me to lend you some?' She swallowed, thinking of how little wages she had left.

'No, thanks anyway.'

'What d'you need it for?'

'For Pam. Buying her a ring, ain't I?'

'Oh, Alfie!' Lillian squealed and the water tipped dangerously close to the sides. 'You getting married?'

'Yeah. Gonna ask her next week – on my birthday. That's why I need it. I ain't got much time.'

'That's smashing,' said Lillian, but her smile faded. 'Pam can wait for a ring, give you time to save up. It's not worth getting into trouble over.'

'I'll be fine ...'

'Or buy her a cheaper ring?'

'She deserves the best.'

'Even so, you shouldn't go back there.'

Alfie began flicking his glove against the sidewall. 'Look, I shouldn't have mentioned it. All I have to do is pick up the cash. If it looks dodgy, I won't go in. All right?'

Lillian sighed. He was three years older than her and she knew from experience there was nothing she could say to make him change his mind.

'Well, make sure Mrs Northcott doesn't catch you up here, she's already got the miff with me.'

'Why? Whatcha do?'

'Not sure. Bit of language in the tearoom, I think.'

Alfie stopped flicking and smiled. For the briefest moment Lillian felt nothing but a rush of happiness for him. Since Pam had been on the scene it felt as though he was finally getting a bit of luck. She held this in mind and tried to ignore the twisted feeling that had crept into the pit of her stomach.

A voice called up from below, 'You up there, Lills?' It was Molly, another counter hand. Alfie put a finger to his lips.

'Just emptying a bowl.'

'Hurry up would ya? Mrs N's on the warpath.'

'Down in a min.' Then to Alfie she whispered, 'Want me to bring you anything?'

'Nah, I'm going now.'

'Take care.'

'Of course.' He began to go back down. Then another voice called up the stairs and they both froze.

'Lillian? Where is that girl?'

She looked Alfie in the eye as the distinct tap of Mrs Northcott's brisk footsteps carried up the tiled stairs.

'Quick,' she whispered. 'She can't know I've been up here talking to you. Go along there and down the other staircase.'

Alfie squeezed round her and crossed the 'Staff Only' sign. She rushed to empty the bowl.

'There you are,' said Mrs Northcott. 'I need to speak to you in the office.'

Lillian followed her up the stairs, still worrying about Alfie, whilst noticing that Mrs Northcott's grey bun was tighter than usual. Once inside the room, Mrs Northcott chose not to sit on the only chair available and the two women, who were about the same height, stood close together in the small space.

'I had a complaint about you earlier.'

'Oh?'

'A lady said you were rude to her boy.'

Lillian remembered his threat. 'I wasn't rude, exactly, he was pretending he had a gun and was shooting me. I asked him to stop.' The mention of a gun caused her to swallow and Mrs Northcott's face grew even sterner.

'It's unacceptable. You have to remember the customer is always in the right. You can't go upsetting little boys who are having tea with their mothers ...'

Lillian flinched at upsetting, thinking of the mess he'd made on the window.

'I know it's hard for you at times. Nasty comments and so forth. But you must learn to button it up and be polite. You're a good worker, but there are plenty of other girls who'd like your job. Besides, it's worth bearing in mind that it wouldn't be easy for you to find something else.'

Lillian nodded. She knew how hard it would be. She'd only got this job because her foster mother had been friendly with someone who worked at the Lyons training school and had arranged the interview.

'It won't happen again.'

'If Mr Clark had been here, well, let's just say he isn't as tolerant as I am.'

'Thank you, Mrs Northcott.'

'Run along now then.'

Lillian gripped the bannisters as she hurried down the stairs.

Molly was busy serving people when she got back to the tearoom. Lillian watched her bouffant hairdo bouncing behind her cap as she bustled about.

'You took your time, having a sneaky fag?' Molly asked.

'Mrs Northcott wanted a word.'

'Tick you off, did she?'

Lillian nodded.

'Don't worry about it. She's a mean old cow sometimes. If she tells me to sort my 'air out one more time, I'm going to tell her what she can do with her bleedin' job. Plenty of cafés want waitresses.'

Lillian mumbled, 'The right kind of waitresses.'

'What was that?'

She spoke louder. 'You can't do that, Molls. Be rubbish here without you.'

'Don't I know it!' Molly grinned at her. The sound of high heels tapped the floor and they both looked towards the door to see who had walked in.

'Vera,' said Molly. 'How's it going?'

'Had me eleven-thirty cancel so I thought I'd pop in here for a quick cuppa.'

'Good timing. We was just talking about me 'air. Can you fit me in Monday for a roots touch-up? I've got an audition.'

'Monday morning? Yeah, no problem. I'll give you a call later.'

'Ta, love. Do you want a French pastry with that?'

'Go on then.'

'Did she call and cancel, or leave you waiting?'

'No, she never bothered. I was staring out the window for fifteen minutes. Won't be booking her again.'

'I wouldn't.'

'Hardly anyone about this morning,' said Vera. 'Must 'ave been the fog. The old lady who works in the shop opposite the salon ain't even bothered opening.'

'That's what Fred from the flower market was saying,' said Lillian, cleaning out the tea urn. 'No one about.' She was running the hot tap to rinse it and had her back to the tearoom but felt a sudden chill as the atmosphere in the room changed. She put the urn down and saw a gang in dark suits had just walked in. One of them wore an expensive-looking plaid overcoat. A woman with platinum-blonde hair and a short purple dress was on his arm. They squeezed round a table that was too small for them, jostling in extra chairs until all six were seated. Their heads leaned in and what must have been a heated discussion began to take place, because fingers were being pointed. The man in the overcoat slammed his hand down on the table top and Lillian jumped.

'You know who that is, don't you?' said Vera. Lillian and Molly shook their heads. 'That's Bill Brunson and his girl, Jackie.' They looked over and saw him gesturing for someone to go and serve them. 'I do Jackie's hair every week. Best go and see what he wants.'

'I don't care who they are,' said Molly. 'They can come to the counter like everyone else.'

'Don't push it, Molls. He's known round 'ere,' said Vera.

Molly picked up a dishcloth and began to polish a glass.

'Go on, will you? I've had to fix Jackie's hair before so her bruises don't show.'

Lillian gulped. 'I'll go,' she said, picking up a menu and walking over. She glanced at Molly, who raised her eyebrows. As she neared the table, she felt her hand begin to tremble, so she put the menu down quickly.

'Hello,' she said. 'How can I help you?'

Bill nodded. 'Appreciate you coming over,' he shot a look at Molly.

Lillian waited while he put a cigarette between his lips and lit it with a square Ronson lighter. She'd seen them before in Lyons but rarely in the hand of someone as young as Bill. He blew out the smoke.

'What's your name?'

'Lillian.'

'Where you from?' he asked.

'Forest Hill,' she said.

There was sniggering around the table and she felt the blood rise to her face.

'Well, Lillian, we've had a bit of a morning, we could all do with a coffee.'

Lillian nodded and picked up the menu, coughing as Bill blew out smoke in the space between them.

Later, as she leant across the table to hand Bill his coffee, she was left stranded mid-air when he didn't reach out to receive it. She looked up and saw him staring at the cup and became conscious, suddenly, of the brownness of her fingers against the porcelain. She put the saucer down and went back behind the counter wondering if she was imagining things.

From across the room she watched their heads huddle together again. Lillian strained her ears to hear if any of it involved a missing gun, but she was too far away and as soon as the conversation rose above a certain level, Bill would tap a key on the table and the volume would die down again.

Jackie stood up and meandered over to talk to Vera. 'How's it going, love?'

'All right, Jackie? Cor, I like your earrings.' Vera lifted a hand and touched one of the large green circles that swung from Jackie's earlobes. Jackie flinched slightly and Vera let go of the earring, she smoothed Jackie's hair back to where it had been before.

The group got up to leave and Lillian picked up a tray to clear the table.

'The sugar needs refilling,' said Bill as he passed her.

'Oh,' said Lillian, rather surprised at his helpfulness. 'Thank you.' But when she lifted up the sugar bowl, she saw something had been scratched into the Formica underneath. She turned her head the other way and made out the wiry letters: 'K.B.W.' Looking up, her eyes met with Bill's whose lip had curled into a snarl. She felt the anger boiling up in her and was about to say something, but at that moment Mrs Northcott walked in the room. She shut her mouth and began clearing the table. She could hear Molly and Vera chatting over by the counter, but their voices were a distant murmur behind the three words that repeated loudly inside her head: Keep Britain White.

Judi Daykin is a professional actor, theatre director, producer and scriptwriter. Her own theatre company, Broad Horizons, specialises in touring new plays recovering and retelling women's history. *Violent Delights* is her first full-length novel. The unfinished ones languish under her desk. Yorkshire born, Judi has lived in Norfolk for nearly forty years.

www.broadhorizonstheatre.co.uk
judidaykinauthor@gmail.com

Violent Delights

It was an overcast night. Much darker than Adam had anticipated. He daren't use a torch as he didn't want to alert the men. There was a strange orange glow in the distance. It hung under the clouds that blotted out the moon. Everyone around here knew that glow. It was the lights at the Bacton Gas Terminal, ever on alert in case of terrorist attack. But it didn't help him now in the slightest.

A pair of those night vision goggles would have been useful, he thought.

Struggling through a gap in the hedge and clambering down into the drainage ditch at the road end of the field, he was already short of breath.

'Not built for this stuff anymore,' he muttered. Not now that retirement and a fondness for real ale had given him a proper belly.

There were several inches of muddy rust-coloured water at the bottom of the ditch. Under the water was a layer of sticky mud trying to pull the wellingtons off his feet. Thank God it had been dry recently, or the disgusting contents would have been much deeper. In spite of the warm night air, the feel of the cold water soaking into his trousers made him shudder.

These ditches cut through many of the farmers' fields in North Norfolk. The waterlogged land needed them. Adam had checked two days ago that this particular one made its way around the edge of the field to the barns that were his target.

Somewhere over to his right, he could hear an irrigator phasing regularly, spitting water out with a snake-like hiss. Salad crops, potatoes, carrots, they'd all be needing a bit of help in this dry spell.

Farming! Who'd have thought it? Not bad for an East End boy, he thought wryly as he struggled along.

It was proving hard going. A sudden slip in the grubby water made him grab at the bank, slicing open his hand on the razor-like edges of the wild grass. He angrily rubbed the blood away on the leg of his jeans. At least here the hedge rose well above the ditch so he could move upright.

When he got near to the barns, there were no hedges. He would have to walk doubled over.

The new camera he'd bought especially for tonight was bouncing off his beer gut as it swung around on its strap. Brambles reached thorny fingers to snatch at the expensive Canon.

Bastard stuff, he thought tugging the camera free. Never mind, it will be worth it.

On his reconnaissance trip, he estimated that it was about half a mile across the fields from the lane to the barns. He had carefully chosen a piece of overgrown scrubland behind a high hedge to leave his car. It should be invisible to passers-by, especially as it was some miles to the nearest village. Only the occasional local would use a minor road like that.

Last night he had parked there and waited in vain, giving up as the August dawn began to grow brighter than the Bacton glow.

Tonight, he returned just before midnight to watch again. Within an hour a solitary vehicle made its way down the road, pausing briefly to drop off three men at the rutted, bumpy cart track which led directly to the weather-worn metal barns. One was carrying a large toolbox.

As soon as the car departed, Adam changed his shoes for wellingtons, hung the camera around his neck and manually locked the car. He left his mobile in the car in case it should ring, never quite confident that he had mastered how to turn the sound off properly. Not fancying his chances against men like these, he couldn't approach from the track. Besides his intention wasn't to tackle them, but to collect real hard evidence. If he was right and could get photos, then he'd prove to a lot of people that he wasn't past it. He grinned at the prospect.

I'll show them I haven't lost my touch, he promised himself as he dragged the camera from the clutch of yet another bramble.

About ten yards from his target the hedge ran out. Although the ditch was at least four feet deep, he had to edge along with his shoulders bent low to prevent his head showing. The camera was swinging wildly to and fro. He steadied it with a muddy hand, then peered cautiously over the edge of the bank.

There were two corrugated iron-clad barns, one larger than the other. They sat at right angles to form a yard area which had been concreted over. Like many farmers in the area, Jack Ellis kept various types of agricultural machinery in barns remote from his house, which was several miles further along the lane.

The doors to the smaller barn stood open. Inside, Adam could see torches flickering here and there against the walls and ceiling. He wriggled his bulk onto the bank to steady himself and the camera.

His investigations had led him to believe that this was organised crime. It was happening all over the region these days, but no one seemed willing or able to find enough evidence to stop it. Furthermore, he had a damn good idea which locals were involved. Well he, Adam Crane, was going to provide all the photographic evidence needed to complete the dossier he had already drawn up.

There was a grinding noise from inside the barn, followed by a clang as something fell to the ground. One of the men was speaking. By the urgency of the voice, he was trying to hurry up the other two, but Adam couldn't make out the exact words. Another of the men opened what sounded like the bonnet of a car. Now all the torches were pointed to the same place, the shadowy figures peering into an engine compartment.

Perhaps I can catch their faces in the torchlight, he thought, taking the lens cap off and placing the camera carefully on the edge of the bank. Zooming in, then focusing as sharply as he could, his finger pressed the shutter button.

Shit, shit, shit.

The camera fired off a series of rapid shots, like paparazzi spotting a film star, the flash going like a strobe.

Urgent voices from the barn made it clear that they'd seen the flickering. Adam's head shot down. He began to struggle back along the ditch, trying hard not to make any noise. After a few terrifying yards, he made it behind the cover of the hedge and slumped against the edge of the ditch.

What a fucking idiot, he berated himself. I spent two bloody days learning how to use the thing. Keep still, keep still.

His heart was pounding, his breath rasping sharply. Surely they would hear it. His chest heaved with fear and unexpected exercise.

Forcing himself to peer through the tangle of vegetation at the base of the hedge, he could see two torches heading out of the barns, shadowy figures behind them. Their movement triggered the outdoor lights fastened above the doors, which blazed across the yard and into the field beyond.

One of the figures began to search towards him on the bank above the ditch; the other was moving in the opposite direction along the cart track. The light from the yard cast an inky-black shadow from the hedge into the ditch. It outlined the men, Adam couldn't see their faces, but it also helped to hide him.

At least he'd had enough sense to wear black clothes, Adam thought.

Knowing that any movement would attract their attention, he fought every instinct to escape. Dropping carefully to one knee in the stinking ditch, he braced himself to escape, crouching like a runner in starting blocks. The repulsive water soaked into his trousers making them hang heavily from their belt and stick to his legs. He shivered as he waited.

Halting at the hedge, the man shone his torch around. Adam tried to hold his breath. The yard lights timed out, then cut in again, as the searcher walked back along the top of the ditch.

I've got away with it, Adam thought as he took a deep breath. Fuck, that was close.

Then the man kicked something in the grass and bent down to check. Holding it up to examine in the light from his torch, he suddenly whistled a high piercing note, beckoning to the other on the cart track who returned. The item was handed over.

'Camera lens cap. Someone's spying on us. Can't have gone far.'

The second man didn't reply. Instead, he swung his torch around, searching the ditch and field beyond. The beam passed just inches above Adam's head. Without further words, they began to walk along the ditch, one in each direction, shining their torches up and down like searchlights in a prison.

Fear galvanised Adam. He shot upright and began to race along the ditch like a startled animal, spattering water wildly, not caring about the racket he was making. The men must have heard him bolt. With a yell, one jumped into the ditch and started to chase after him.

Sheer panic engulfed Adam, flooding him with extra adrenalin as he lumbered along. He had never been more afraid in his sixty-five years, not even on riot duty. The pursuer seemed to be gaining on him until there was a sharp cry, followed by a sudden splash. Elated, but terrified, Adam hoped the man had tripped on the same brambles he was struggling against. It gave him a slim chance.

An engine turned over. Someone had managed to get the vehicle started. Headlights flicked on. A Land Rover Defender drove out of the barn at speed.

'Come back,' Adam heard the man on the bank shout to the pursuer. 'Faster in the Landie.'

He'd be safer in the middle of the fields, Adam knew, harder to find. Besides, they'd be armed, these types always were.

He struggled on. His chest felt like it was bound with a steel band as he drew short agony-filled breaths. The mud was pinning his boots down in the bottom of the ditch. His thighs burned with the effort of pulling them out. Red flashes clouded his vision. Pounding filled his ears. The slime suddenly sucked away one wellington. Not daring to turn back to retrieve it, he hobbled manically on.

The rubbish in the bottom of the ditch sliced into the sole of his foot. The overgrown grasses lacerated his arms and face and legs. Brambles snatched at his clothes like demon fingers trying to hold him back. He tore them loose. Struggling in terror, and almost blinded with effort, Adam lurched into a bank wall. It was a dead end. He must have taken a wrong turn into one of the connecting ditches. He slid down the bank in despair. Everything was hurting.

Above the sound of his gasping, he could hear the engine running in the distance. The men were arguing, using their torches to scan the field. Looking for him. The headlights began to bounce out of the yard and along the track towards the main road. His wrong turning had brought him close to the track. Too close. There were no hedges here to protect him.

He crawled frantically away from the track on his hands and knees, then burrowed underneath a thick patch of undergrowth at the bottom of the ditch. As he lay on his side in the stinking red mud, stretching his neck to keep his face out of the water, he willed his breathing to recover. Keeping as still as he could, he listened hard. The vehicle drove along the track, stopping every few yards, the men climbing out and using their torches to scan the fields and ditches. He almost pissed himself as they moved past. Not that anyone would be able to notice, he was completely soaked.

But in spite of their thoroughness, they missed him.

Eventually, the men reached the road. After a short, furious argument, they seemed to give up. The vehicle doors slammed, and Adam heard it drive off along the narrow lane towards Happisburgh.

He lay in the vile water for a long time, until he began to shake with cold and shock. Slowly he edged from underneath the cover to crawl up the bank of the ditch. Checking cautiously over the top, he made sure that there was no one to be seen in the gloomy night. No silent guard left to wait for him.

Exhausted, he stumbled up onto the track. His arms, hands, face, feet and legs were covered with scratches, cuts and bruises. His clothes were soaked, blood-spattered and ripped. There wasn't any point in trying to hide now. They had gone, thank God. He began to limp along the track to the lane and his car.

The new camera was still on its strap, but it was smashed and dripping blood-red water. There would be little chance of salvaging any pictures.

'I'll pay for this tomorrow,' Adam grumbled, hobbling along. 'I'm bloody paying for it now.'

The road was rough under his bootless foot, making him wince with every step. Nearing the gap in the hedge where he had hidden his car, he fumbled with bloodied and unco-operative fingers in his trouser pocket for the car keys.

Then, without warning, headlights blinded him.

CHAPTER TWO

It felt like a release, being able to close the door to her very own flat for the first time in her life. As if Sara were shutting out the past, putting a full stop to the bitter argument that had raged between herself and her mother for weeks now.

Downstairs, the front door slammed. She went out onto the small wooden-decked balcony to look down. In the street, three storeys below, a handsome young man turned to look up at her and waved.

They had met at lunchtime. Sara and her step-father were struggling to carry a huge box upstairs, Chris coming home for a break. Dumping his coat in the flat one floor below, her new neighbour had helped them carry her possessions up the three flights for an hour or more. He didn't shy away from hard work. Once the last box was upstairs, Chris had taken them across the road for lunch in the independent coffee shop which he was proud to own and run.

He might be considered handsome, Sara thought watching him now, with his neatly trimmed trendy beard and curly brown hair cropped close around his ears.

She was taller than him, but then she was taller than many people. This evening he knocked on the door and offered to fetch a pizza after her long day of moving in. At first, she had declined. But he gently persisted, so she accepted. He seemed a nice guy if a bit over-keen. But then he didn't know she was a police officer yet.

For a moment, Sara allowed herself to admire the view across the rooftops of central Norwich. Away to the left, the Cathedral spire rose above the city, as it must have done for centuries. A castle floated above the houses too, as if by magic. The place had an aura of gentility and middle-class wealth. Down in the narrow street, there were surprisingly few vehicles for a Saturday evening. She could see several restaurants, Chris's café, a variety of fashionable shops and plenty of people.

The warm August air rose gently up, bringing the scent of Norwich with it. Garlic from the restaurant kitchens, fresh ground coffee from the café, an overlay of something green from the nearby park. Perhaps they had recently cut the grass. The whole place seemed quaint in comparison to Tower Hamlets and the family home she shared with Tegan, her mother.

There the houses crowded up to one another; cars occupied every available space; the rumble of traffic always in the background. Some days, especially hot ones like today, the London aroma combined over-flowing rubbish bins with traffic pollution or the temporary urinal of an alley next to her mum's ex-council maisonette. Other days, a fresh breeze would blow up from the Thames dockside just a few streets away, filling the air with cleansing river ozone. It had been her home for the last thirty-four years.

No doubt there would be a darker side to the place. Otherwise, there wouldn't be any work for her to do. It remained to be seen if Norwich would come to feel like home in the future.

Turning back into the living room, she sighed. There was packing debris all over the place. Somewhere underneath all this junk, her new IKEA sofa and coffee table were lurking. It was going to take a lot of tidying up, but it could wait. She was exhausted. Perhaps the pizza was a good idea after all.

The bedroom was in better shape. Her new bed, a hopeful double, was made up, ready for the moment when she needed to collapse and sleep. Her largest suitcase was waiting on top. Inside, there was something she needed to find. Pulling aside the clothes, Sara came to her treasure. A tin box.

With care, she carried it into the living room. Sweeping aside the cardboard and plastic, to unearth the table and make a space on the sofa to sit down, she placed the tin in the middle of the table, briefly laying a hand on the lid, as if comforting an animal.

Originally a deep royal blue, now the colour was fading. There was Oriental lettering and decoration around the wall of the tin. On the lid was a scratched but pretty scene embossed in gold colouring. It showed two long-legged birds performing what she hoped was a mating dance, rather than a fight. The tin looked out of place on the modern table.

Perhaps it had once held biscuits, or expensive chocolates or a precious gift of some sort. Now she looked at it with such reverence, that it might as well have held a family member's ashes. But it didn't. The contents were simple but explosive. A handful of letters and a few old photographs. All those arguments, this radical upheaval, had been because of a few scraps of paper.

I know I'm doing the right thing, she assured herself. It will all be good in the end. It has to be.

And to think it had all started with a theft.

Sara had found the blue box six months previously, at the back of her mother's wardrobe. She hadn't been searching for it, hadn't even suspected it existed. She'd been looking for an old handbag Tegan asked her to find. They were heading out that evening to an '80s night at the local pub, and Tegan wanted to dress the part, put on the glad rags from her youth.

Intrigued, Sara had opened it to find a few handwritten letters stuffed into their original envelopes and some photos, which were beginning to fade and discolour. Feeling guilty, she took the tin to her bedroom. Unpacking the contents, she read them swiftly the first time, more slowly the second. Then she repacked the tin and hid it.

It had been the start of all this drastic change, the key to a question which her mother steadfastly refused to answer.

She'd shared a home with her mother and grandfather for as long as she could remember, but no father or grandmother. Grandma had passed away when Sara was three years old, and she had no recollection of her, though there were plenty of photos to look at. But the absence of her father was forbidden territory.

'Where's my daddy?' she had once asked coming in from infant school, where her friends had asked her the same question.

Her granddad's reply had been to smack her. The only time he had ever done so. She hadn't asked him again.

As a teenager, becoming aware that her skin colour was lighter than either her mum's or her Jamaican granddad's drove her curiosity. One awkward afternoon after school she had taken Tegan to a coffee bar, where Granddad wouldn't hear them and asked again.

'Who was my dad? Where did he go?'

'Why would you want to know all about that?' her Mum sounded hurt. 'Don't we look after you good enough?'

'Of course you do. But why am I so much lighter than you?' She laid her arm next to her mother's on the Formica table.

For a while, Tegan stared out of the café window into the busy street, then said, 'If I tell you, you can't ask Granddad about it, OK?'

'I promise.'

'He was a whitey. No good white boy.'

Sara waited, but nothing else seemed to be forthcoming.

'So what happened?' she prompted.

'You don't need to know,' her mother said angrily. 'He no good to me, to our family. Stop asking.'

As she matured into a woman, Sara began to wonder if her mother had either had an affair or if it was even worse. Perhaps she had been threatened or raped.

She never raised the issue again. It was obviously too painful. Why should Sara's curiosity mean that her mum would have to relive something she wanted to forget? She loved her mum and granddad, in spite of the differences of opinion they might sometimes have. Let sleeping secrets lie and all that.

Having no visible father or being of dual heritage simply wasn't that big a deal in her multi-cultural neighbourhood. It hadn't stopped her succeeding at school, getting a good place at university or joining the Metropolitan Police. Hard work had been the key.

If she felt the occasional hazing she was subjected to at work did have racist overtones, then it wasn't overt enough to complain. Not that Sara was the complaining type. Everyone got hazed now and then; it was a camaraderie thing. She was resilient enough to sort it out herself. She knew she'd earned her promotion to Detective Sergeant, and she was proud of it.

Then all her certainties, those decisions to forget, had been undermined by a blue tin. For weeks she had debated confronting her mother with this new knowledge but realised that it would cause a fight and Tegan had enough on her plate. Granddad was succumbing to Alzheimer's; they'd placed him in a nursing home. It made her mum feel guilty. There was no point in opening old wounds.

Damn it all, she decided, I call myself a detective. I'll investigate it privately.

Simple internet searches had yielded little that was helpful. The letters were signed 'A' and had been posted from Norwich in the 1980s. A search of the census documents from the area yielded hundreds of men with appropriate ages and a first name beginning with 'A'. She could never track them all down.

It was obvious from the contents that 'A' had been a policeman who had moved from the Met to the Norwich force. She had made a vague attempt to interrogate personnel files in the office but knew she was only drawing unwelcome attention to herself.

Sara read and re-read the letters until she knew them by heart. She studied the pictures until she thought her eyes might burn them to dust.

They jumped into her thoughts unbidden when she was at work. The grainy image of the man whom she now presumed to be her dad troubled her dreams. Finally, she accepted that she would have to find another way to solve the mystery. To try to track down her father, before her lack of knowledge damaged the rest of her life.

Because the letters didn't speak of an illicit affair or a shocking rape. They were love letters.

Tegan had gone ballistic when Sara had announced plans to move to Norwich and join the Norfolk Police's Serious Crimes Unit.

'I don't see why you have to go. What's wrong with what you're doing here?'

'I want a place of my own.'

'You could get a place here. Why go there?'

'I can't afford anything here. You know that. Besides, it's a good promotion. I'll be in a smaller team. I can make a bigger impact. Do more good.'

She didn't dare tell her mum that she had been offered an even better promotion in the Met. When she had returned from her interview in Norfolk, a hasty conversation at the Yard had elicited an offer to move into Anti-Terrorism. The Personnel Manager couldn't understand why Sara turned that down.

'You're throwing away all your efforts and going to that dump of a place. Why?' Sweat began to break out on Tegan's face; tears welled up.

'It's what I want, Mum.'

'Then why not another big city? Better opportunities?'

Sara didn't answer.

'I can't bear it. After all we do, to get you through university. All those endless shifts your granddad did to help with the money. All that hair I wash and cut and pamper, just so you don't have to. Now, you throw it all away.'

Her mother's partner, Javed, sat beside her on the sofa. He was a kind man, Sara liked him. He tried to pull Tegan into a calming hug, crooning 'Come on baby, calm down.'

Tegan struggled free, stood up and turned on Sara, rigid with anger.

'If you do this, if you throw all that work back in our faces, I will never speak to you again.'

She'd stormed out of the house, taking her coat and bag with her.

'What have you done?' Javed asked Sara with a sigh. 'You know how weird she be about that place. I thought she would throw me out one time I suggest we go holiday there.'

When Tegan failed to return, Sara and Javed went to the salon Tegan ran with her best friend on Cable Street.

She hadn't been there all day, Ali assured them.

The pair spent the rest of the afternoon searching Tegan's favourite places. The Caribbean Café, the Tower Hamlets Social Club, the Taste of Jamaica Restaurant. No one had seen her. Hours after the shops closed, they returned to the salon and found her sitting in the small kitchen at the back.

'Come on, love,' Javed tried to take her hand, but Tegan snatched it away. 'It up to Sara what she do with her life.'

'Like I ever had any choice. I did what I have to do. You don't understand, girl. I wanted you to be free.'

'But I am free, Mum, and this is my own choice.'

'You think you've had it bad here, been passed over for the better jobs 'cos of your heritage? You wait until you get up there.'

'My heritage? I don't know what my heritage is.'

'You have me. You have Granddad. What more do you want?'

'Let's leave Granddad out of this,' Sara was getting angry.

'Why? Just because he's in a home now?' Tegan rounded on her daughter. 'You think it don't matter no more, what he do for you? Just because he not always recognise you when ya' bother to visit?'

'He doesn't recognise either of us.'

'He looked after us both, plenty good. You ungrateful, you don't-care-girl. You talk big, doin' famous job. No time for your family.'

'That's unfair, Mum.'

'I think we should all take a break,' Javed had nodded at Sara to leave the room, which she'd been glad to do.

They always ended up fighting if they talked about Granddad. Just like Sara had frequently argued with him when he was still living in the maisonette. Before his Alzheimer's had taken hold.

For four more weeks, they had tiptoed around each other, nursing their anger along with their secrets, Javed trying to act as a mediator. Once the boxes had started filling, the lease on the flat in Norwich was signed and the move inevitable, her mother lapsed into complete silence, refusing to help at all. Exasperated, Javed had defied Tegan for once and hired a van to help Sara move, before it all became too unbearable.

So here she was in Norwich. She patted the blue tin again as if to assure herself it was still there. After all, moving here might be little more than a romantic notion of following in her father's footsteps.

All Sara knew was that her instinct told her that she could do more here, and a good copper always listened to their instinct. Perhaps she would spend her spare days going through local rates records or newspapers from the period. Just maybe the personnel files would be easier to access here than in the Met.

One thing was for certain, whatever the outcome of her search, her immediate priority would be to settle into her new team. First impressions always count, so on Monday morning, she would have to be on her best form.

The downstairs door slammed shut again. Footsteps climbed the stairs; there was a knock at the door.

Yes, I have to make it worth the gamble, she thought, patting the tin again.

'Pizza delivery,' called Chris's friendly voice. Sara opened the door and let him in.

Antony Dunford divides his time between Hertfordshire, London, and Yorkshire. His short story *The Princess Beatrice*, describing the meeting of a Punjabi soldier and an Australian pilot during the siege of Kut in 1915, was runner-up in the *Away from the Western Front* competition commemorating the centenary of the end of the Great War. *Hunted* is his first novel.

antony.dunford@effortfreelife.com

Hunted

CHAPTER ONE

The dream wasn't a dream. It was a memory. The street so bright; the buildings as insubstantial as thoughts; the smile on the face of that man; that smile; the quiet. Then the explosion, her head brutally stuffed with white noise and deafening light as smile became the last thing that man ever did. But it wasn't the dream that wasn't a dream that woke her, breathless and gasping for air, as if she'd been suffocated.

Cold sweat. She slept in a thin, sleeveless T-shirt and shorts under a single thin sheet. She wasn't hot. The air-con did its job keeping out the heat of Kenya's endless summer. But she was covered in cold, clammy sweat. The first time in many months.

She realised her eyes were open.

The day was still out there. Sunlight sneaked around the edges of the blinds. Her shift had finished at six in the morning. She had gone to bed at eight. Her alarm had not gone off yet. It was set for four. Nightshifts turned the world inside out.

She reached for her phone on the bedside stand next to her hand gun. Three o'clock. A missed call. Was that what had woken her? Two minutes ago. Annick. Her sister.

As she looked at the screen a text message beeped in.

Ring umiddelbart. Call immediately.

She pressed the call button.

'Mr Short is dead,' Annick said. *Er død.*

She did not respond.

'Jane, are you there? Did you hear me? Steve is dead.'

'I heard you,' Jane said. She closed her eyes.

—

Steve Short was a huge man. Tall, broad, and with a spare tyre around his waist. 'Fat as a hippo's arse,' he used to describe himself, before bursting out laughing, usually with a barbecued chicken leg in one hand and a bottle of beer in the other. He was so large he had to go to Nairobi, or back home to Johannesburg, to buy his clothes.

He had been found that morning by his wife on her return from a trip into Nanyuki. On the veranda, collapsed in a great heap, one huge hand still gripping a wooden post, the other across his chest as if reaching for his heart. His eyes closed and still warm. The doctor said heart attack. He was fifty-seven.

In death, at least only a few hours after his death, he seemed undiminished. He was so tall his dining room table was not long enough to lay him out on. The six men who carried him inside had dragged his beloved card table over and rested his head on that. He looked peaceful, as though enjoying one last sunset. But his skin was turning purple. He was undeniably dead. Jane reached out her hand to his face but let it fall without touching.

Annick put her hand on Jane's shoulder, gently, like a resting bird.

The only sound was the soft sobbing of Naomi, Steve's wife. Naomi hadn't taken her eyes off Steve's face since Jane and Annick had been shown into the room. She held a brightly-coloured scarf to her mouth as her tears ran.

Then there was another sound from outside the dining room window. A low growl that turned into a roar.

'That's a very big lion,' Jane said.

'That's not a lion. That's an elephant. An elephant in distress,' said Annick.

The sound came again, but this time a second one overlapped it, and then a third.

Jane followed Annick out onto the veranda where Nathan and Timu, the other two rangers on Jane's shift, were already watching in amazement.

Tony Kanagi, the Conservancy's chief ranger, was about twenty metres out from the veranda, cowering by the door of the Land Cruiser he must have just parked at the end of the line of four similar vehicles.

The roar came again, two, three, four, a dozen times. A wall of sound. The Conservancy's herd of elephants, all fifteen of them, were surrounding Kanagi's vehicle on three sides, though his presence seemed incidental as their attention was on the ranch. They stepped from foot to foot, raised their heads, pointed their trunks to the setting sun, and roared, not in unison, but one at a time. It was deeper, older, and more powerful than the roar of any lion Jane had heard. The sound ached with loss.

'They are saying goodbye,' Naomi said. 'They are saying goodbye to Steve.'

Jane had not noticed her follow them onto the veranda. Naomi's tears had stopped, and she was smiling, though her eyes were as red as the setting sun.

'Thank you, Bibi,' Naomi said, loudly. The men looked at her in surprise. Jane and Annick were watching Bibi, the oldest female elephant in the herd. She had been leading the pacing, the movement from foot to foot, the strange dance the herd stepped and repeated. When Naomi spoke the elephant stopped, stood still, looked straight at the woman half her height and a tiny fraction of her size. She flicked her ears, blinked her eyes, and briefly lowered her head. Then she made a different sound, a low-frequency rumble like the creaking of snow before an avalanche. The other elephants stopped their roars and waited. Bibi turned to her right, walking past Major Kanagi's car, brushing it with her foreleg.

Others of the herd bashed into the car too as they left. Major Kanagi, moved as the vehicle was turned, crouching his way round the back to avoid being hit by both the car and the massive animals. The last to trot past was a baby, no more than a few months old. As he passed, he raised his tail and let drop his afternoon dung.

Eventually the elephants were lost away to the west in a cloud of dust, and the front of Tony Kanagi's car was scrap metal. None of the other cars had been touched. The air smelt of elephant.

Kanagi stood up, did his best to beat the dust out of his uniform, and marched with dignity towards the veranda. He put his foot in the pile of droppings on his third step. With barely a pause he strode on, reached the veranda, climbed the steps, and stood in front of Naomi.

'My sincerest condolences to you, Mrs Short. Today the Conservancy has lost its father,' he said, whilst surreptitiously trying to scrape the dung off his boot on the edge of the step.

'Thank you, Major,' Naomi said. Tony Kanagi claimed he had been a major in the Kenyan army. Some of the rangers believed he was exaggerating.

'I will be happy to take charge of the day-to-day running of things until you decide what it is you will do,' Kanagi said. Jane watched him and Naomi more closely.

'I haven't even – I mean, there's – I,' Naomi took a deep breath, blinking back tears. 'Thank you, Major,' she said eventually. She turned back into the ranch and closed the door.

'Jennings, Obote, Haven, you are on shift tomorrow at two p.m., do not be late,' Kanagi said as soon as the door was shut.

'Our shift starts at ten p.m. tonight,' Jane said.

'Your shift starts at two p.m. tomorrow afternoon,' he repeated. 'You heard Mrs Short. I am in charge now.'

The Major marched down the steps. He had evidently forgotten the state of his vehicle. He turned back to those on the veranda.

'Haven, give me your keys,' he snapped.

Jane stared at him, her face like basalt.

'Your keys,' he snapped again, clicking his fingers.

'You can have my keys, boss,' said Timu Obote, the youngest of the rangers. He was scrabbling in his pocket for the keys to the Conservancy Land Rover he'd driven to the ranch.

'I said Haven. Keys, now,' Kanagi clicked his fingers three more times in Jane's direction. She crossed her arms and set her feet apart. Annick stepped back. Nathan Jennings, the other ranger, was watching Jane with a blank expression.

For a moment time seemed to stand still. Kanagi's arm outstretched, fingers ready to click again; Timu's hands on his many pockets trying to find his keys; Nathan watching; Annick out of sight behind her; Jane ...

Jane was concentrating on not walking up to Kanagi and breaking the arm he was pointing at her in two places.

'Here you go, boss,' Timu said, holding out his hand, the keys to his car in his palm.

The tension broke. Kanagi hesitated, then took the keys. Without looking at Jane he walked to Timu's car, got in, and drove off.

'Oh,' Annick said. 'It's going to be like that, is it?'

'Not for very long,' Jane said.

'Don't hurt him,' Annick said.

'Hurt him?' Timu said, surprise in his voice.

Annick didn't answer. Nathan Jennings was still watching Jane. She turned to look at him. His face was flat, but his eyes were charged.

—

'Do you want to stay at our place tonight?' Annick said. 'He won't mind.'

They were bouncing along the salt-sand road through the Conservancy. The sky was orange with the last of the sun. Away to the north a herd of zebra, peppered with the occasional kudu, corkscrew horns like dead saplings, grazed warily in the dying light. A zebra mare gave a cautious snort. As if in answer, the first evening roar of a waking pride of lions came from a few kilometres to the south.

'No. I need to be on shift tonight,' Jane said.

'Kanagi said you were on shift tomorrow.'

'And that doesn't have you curious? Seven hours after Steve dies, he switches the next shift for no reason.'

'He just wants to prove he's in charge. That he can control the white woman!' Annick said 'white woman' the way teenagers around campfires at midnight say 'mad axeman'.

'That's not enough,' Jane said.

'It is for him! Three years of complaining to Steve about a woman ranger! "There are no other ranger women in Africa",' Annick said, in a passable imitation of Kanagi's voice.

Jane smiled at that. Not at Kanagi's complaint, nor at the memory of Steve's responses, every one different: 'Explains why there's so much poaching' had been her favourite. No, she smiled because each time Steve heard she'd suffered Kanagi's insults he would come and bring her fruit and reason with her not to put Kanagi in his place. 'You need to be the bigger man, here,' Steve would say, a twinkle in his eye.

'It's not enough,' Jane said to Annick, not taking her eyes off the road.

They had reached the edge of the Conservancy where the electric fence had a tall and imposing wooden gate in front of it. At least it was tall and looked imposing. It wouldn't have kept a gazelle in, if it hadn't been for the far less imposing but much more effective steel gate inside it. The wooden one was for the tourists. 'Waste of bloody money,' Steve had said, but Naomi had been firm. It looked like the gate from a film. It would add to their revenues.

Steve had not cared about revenues, just animals. Jane had learnt so much from him.

She drove back to her apartment where Annick had left her car. Annick got out, came around, and gave Jane an imperfect hug through the open window.

'You be safe, little sister,' Annick said. Jane smiled.

'Aren't I always?'

Jane put the car into gear and pulled away. She glanced in the rear-view mirror and thought she saw Annick mouth 'No'.

Night was shroud-black by the time she pulled up to the gate of the inner conservancy behind Festo's Land Rover. Festo was Kiga, from Uganda, almost as much of an outcast from the other rangers as she was. He wasn't of the Kamba. But he had a way about him, and the two other rangers on his shift respected him.

He got out of his car, opened the gates, watched it drive through, and waited for her to follow.

Once through he shut the gates behind her. She let the engine idle as he walked over.

'A day of great sadness,' Festo said.

'A day of great sadness,' she repeated.

'The Major switched our shifts.'

'I know. I want to see Douglas. On my own time,' Jane said.

Festo nodded. He walked back to his car and got in. The two Kamba rangers of his shift were inside, one driving, the other in the back. Jane waited for him to set off then followed, the headlights of the two vehicles the only light beneath the stars.

After about a kilometre Festo's driver stopped next to a third vehicle parked beneath a lone acacia. Jane pulled up beside them. Festo and the two Kamba got out, checked their assault rifles, and pulled on their packs with food, water and equipment for the next eight hours. Festo also carried a broom, the bristles on the end worn and dusty.

Jane heard a crackle over her short-wave radio.

'Warthog tree, Last Lion Rock.' That was where the rhinos and their guards were. The females would be together. Douglas would be alone.

The two Kamba set out towards the south west, infrared goggles on. Festo set out north west, towards the Warthog tree, carrying the broom handle. Jane followed him taking only her own infrared goggles.

Festo didn't bother with goggles. He seemed to know his way in pitch black. His rifle was slung across his pack, and he used the broom-handle as a walking staff. He strode at pace with complete confidence. Jane had to use her goggles to see where he was going. She followed.

After five hundred metres a call came through the dark.

'*Wewe ni nani?*'

Who are you? In Swahili, rather than in Kikamba. The ranger on duty accepted Festo as a colleague.

'*Festo, siku hii ya kusikitisha,*' Festo said. Festo, on this sad day.

'*Hii ni siku ya kusikitisha,*' came the reply.

The shift-switch was quick. A nothing-to-report, a handshake, a brief explanation of where Douglas was, and the other ranger was gone back to the vehicles.

As his footsteps were absorbed by the night a silence expanded.

It did not last long. Far away a lion roared. Here, in the inner conservancy, there were no lions. Just three rhinoceroses.

The ground started to shake, as if a squad of soldiers was marching in step towards them. Thump, thump, thump.

Despite knowing what was happening, Jane's heart began to race. The something thumping towards them through the dark was three tonnes of bad-tempered rhinoceros. Any sensible person would find a tree, climb it, and hope that the rhinoceros didn't decide to knock it down.

She saw him emerge from the night.

Douglas was forty-six, not bad for a rhinoceros. Armour-plated and fat from good-living. He'd smelt Festo. He may have smelt her too, but he didn't care about her. He cared about Festo.

The infrared goggles showed Douglas in a green light. He wasn't at full speed, which was close to fifty kilometres an hour and terrifying to witness. He was lumbering. But even lumbering he was impressive. His wide head and wider body, from a distance in proportion, seemed impossibly large up close. His shoulder was nearly two metres off the ground, taller than Festo.

Three years Jane had guarded him, eight hours a day, a day off each week, two days off every other week. And he never ceased to terrify her. It was like being approached by a hungry tank.

Through her goggles she saw Festo calmly take his pack off, place it on the ground, and walk towards the trotting animal, broom-handle twirling.

Douglas should have had a sixty-centimetre horn protruding from the end of his nose. But it had been removed, cut off so that he wouldn't be a target for poachers tempted by the compressed hair that was worth much more than its weight in gold on the black market in Vietnam.

The gap between Douglas and Festo was narrowing rapidly. But the rhino was slowing. Instead of lowering his head for battle he was raising it in greeting. He made a sound not dissimilar to a horse's whinny. When he was twenty metres from Festo, Douglas stopped completely and waited. Festo span the broom handle again.

'*Jioni nzuri, rafiki yangu,*' Festo said. Good evening, my friend.

As Douglas stood still Festo reached forward and scratched the rhinoceros's great belly and inside his legs with the broom handle. Douglas gave a snort of what could only be satisfaction. Jane watched. She'd seen this a hundred times, but she still felt her cheeks flush and her eyes prickle.

At the end of this sad day, Douglas, the last male Northern White Rhino alive, was in good hands.

CHAPTER TWO

The next morning Jane awoke to the sounds of Nanyuki. Shouts in the street outside her apartment, traffic on the main road half a kilometre away, birdsong both wild and domestic. Amongst the birds she recognised two voices: the strangely-hypnotic cheeky robot call of the Splendid Glossy Starling, and the incessant crowing of a neighbour's mad cockerel. The cockerel not only crowed to welcome the sun each morning, but kept crowing to welcome everything else, and continued crowing through the day until he was crowing to let everyone know it was time to go to sleep. Not for the first time she imagined strangling him.

Then she remembered Steve Short was dead and that the world of today was very different to the world of yesterday.

Memories of Steve with the animals ran through her mind. He'd been passionate about all creatures, from the wildest to the tamest. He had spent time with the rhinos, but he'd seen them as much more Annick's territory. He had been particularly smitten with that funny little stray dog a couple of years ago, until it was eaten by a crocodile. But the elephants were his love. Steve in his Land Rover, Bibi's trunk through the window, sniffing him. Steve and some of the rangers pulling a baby elephant out of a narrow gully it had fallen into. Steve's huge laugh whilst playing cards with herself, Annick, and Naomi. Steve's face as he lay dead on his dining room table, his head on the card table, his sparkling eyes closed.

Fuzzy from the shock of grief and erratic sleep she cleared her head with a ten-kilometre run through the maze-like back tracks of Nanyuki, crossing the equator four times. Then a short, hot shower. After dressing in her fatigues, she ate spiced rice for breakfast, a foodstuff once so alien and now her regular fare. She left the apartment far too early to drive straight to the Conservancy and start her shift. She put on her sunglasses, got in the car and set off anyway, undecided as to how she would spend the extra time.

She drove through Nanyuki, heading in the direction she needed to go but in no hurry. Traffic was heavier than usual, the tail end of the morning rush as the shop-owners drove in before the ranchers came in to do their shopping. She was soon through it and heading out of town on the C76 road into Laikipia County where the Conservancy was. She passed the sewage plant and the small airport. A plane was coming in to land, a sleek private jet, probably bringing some wealthy westerner for a safari or a hunting trip.

The Graveyard was coming up on the left, half a kilometre off the road on the track to the north-eastern entrance to the Conservancy. There were no bodies buried there, but one stone had been placed for each rhino, elephant, lion, and hippo taken from the sanctuary by poachers and trophy hunters in the last twenty years. There were hundreds of them, thousands of them.

On instinct Jane turned the wheel and pulled in. She stopped the car, got out and walked across the dry earth to the Graveyard, her heart rate quickening as it always did as the number of stones, many carved with names or places or dates or all three, became clear. She kept walking until she was amongst them, at the heart of desolation.

She squatted in the dust and read some of the stones at random. 'Heidi,' one simply said. 'Male elephant 22.09.02' said another. '*rinoceros nyeusi* Feb8'. 'Three lioness 04.2004. They took their bones.' '*familia ya tembo Mwaka mpya* 2010'. Family of elephants, New Year 2010.

Steve Short had given most of his being to slowing the rate at which stones appeared here. The rest of it he'd given to beer, cards, and barbecued chicken.

At the centre of the Graveyard was a fever tree, one of the mighty acacia that rose from the arid landscape like sentinels of hope. Some of the rangers, including Jane, made a scratch in the bark each time a poacher was caught or killed, keeping score. There were a healthy number now, to the detriment of the tree's health. But there were always more poachers, and always fewer animals.

The Graveyard stood in an area that had once been a British prisoner-of-war camp. Ten thousand Italians captured in Abyssinia and held until 1944; a larger population than that of modern Nanyuki.

Back then rhinos and elephants had roamed free on the slopes of Mount Kenya and the biggest population of man for hundreds of kilometres had been kept behind fences. Seventy years on and the most dangerous thing on Mount Kenya was the mountain itself. The surviving animals were the ones behind fences.

Steve had called the Conservancy *Patakatifu*. It had taken Jane several days to learn how to pronounce it when she spoke no Swahili and it sounded like nothing she'd ever heard. 'Pat a cat if you' had helped. *Patakatifu*. The Sanctuary. At least that's what he'd tried to make it. She would keep trying. Even if she hadn't found her own peace here, she owed it to Steve. She'd been empty when she arrived, but he'd welcomed her as part of his family without hesitation or judgement.

Jane put her hand on the bark of the tree and felt the six scratches, still fresh-looking, she'd made most recently. She watched her fingers trace their shape, then looked away. She stared out across the stones and up at the distant mountain rising into the clouds. She was lost again now. A single living thing in a vastness of living things, all being hunted, all fighting for their own survival. She stood motionless for some minutes, until she shook herself out of her thoughts. She determined to lose herself in her job, for now. She walked to the car without looking back.

She drove back to the C76 and followed it west. The animals in the county avoided the tarmacked roads, and under the morning sun nothing living seemed to move but for the cars; metal beetles crawling through the rising heat. After half an hour she reached the turning to the main Conservancy entrance and drove through the ostentatious gate.

She was still early, an uncomfortable feeling. She lived her life to a timetable, alarms and alerts. This listless wandering wasn't right. She wasn't sure if it was caused by Steve's death. Or by Kanagi changing her shift at short notice without reason. There had to be a reason. Just to prove he could, that wasn't enough. Was it?

But as soon as she was inside the Conservancy she relaxed, gripped the steering wheel less tightly. This place was definitely her home now.

She drove to the main building to see Annick. Farashuu, one of the administrators, said she was with the chimps.

The enclosure in which the chimps were kept was a little away from the main building. Jane jogged there, just because walking seemed too slow.

The security on the chimp enclosure was significant, mainly because chimps can climb. Double fences with anti-climb tops. The trees were kept trimmed so there was a large gap between them and the fences. There was a raised walkway around the outside for tourists, protected by a Perspex screen, because chimps can throw and are ferociously territorial. Jane climbed the stairs to the walkway and looked into the enclosure.

She could see a couple of the primates. One was picking insects out of the other's fur. There were nearly twenty in there somewhere, but the rest were keeping out of sight. They weren't native to Kenya, but a chimp sanctuary in Uganda had run out of funding and Steve had opened his doors after convincing his investors of the tourist-friendly pull of a bunch of cheeky chimps. Well, Naomi had done the soft sell.

A third chimp, a mother with a baby on her back, emerged from behind the trunk of a tree. The baby's eyes watched everything with surprise and sometimes delight.

But Annick wasn't there.

Jane watched for a few more minutes then headed over to the inner reserve and the start of her shift.

—

Kanagi was waiting for her at the gate to the inner reserve. He'd never done that before. Jennings and Obote were with him. They were early. Obote particularly was never early, usually arriving in a cloud of apologies after the handover.

'Poacher sighting, north. Check it out,' Kanagi said to her before she'd even got out of her car. He wore dark jungle fatigues, not the desert fatigues the rest of the rangers favoured. And mirrored sunglasses. It was difficult to see him beyond a cliché. His expression was unreadable. Jennings and Obote were silent. Obote stood slightly awkwardly, as if consciously trying not to think about the way he was stood. He looked nervous.

'I'm on shift,' Jane said.

'Once you've checked out the report. Jennings and Obote will remain with the animals.'

'What report?'

'A sighting of armed men near the army barracks. And a camp fire on ranch land.' Kanagi held out a piece of paper.

'Poachers went near the army barracks and lit a camp fire? Doesn't sound like poachers,' Jane said, ignoring the proffered paper. A kilometre or so behind the three men inside the fence she could see a vehicle parked. The rangers on shift would be nearby, protecting the rhinos.

'They were seen carrying tusks,' Jennings said, unexpectedly to Kanagi, judging by a flash-change in his expression. Jane looked closely at Jennings's face. His sunglasses weren't mirrored, but they were very dark. His mouth gave nothing away.

She reached out for the paper. The handwriting was atrocious and the note was written in Swahili. *Jangili*. Was that a word used for poacher? There were a few and she couldn't remember them all. Next to the word were written some co-ordinates, latitude and longitude.

'Who phoned it in?' Jane said.

'A man,' said Kanagi. He turned his back to her, evidently done with the conversation. Jennings was already moving to open the inner Conservancy gate.

Jane didn't like it. Not one bit. It did not smell right. There was a choice. Do as she was told, follow up a lead that sounded false – especially Jennings saying poachers were seen carrying tusks. She would have heard of elephants taken from any of the parks, reserves or conservancies on the plateau. There was a network of communications, there were drones patrolling hundreds of miles with sensors that reported on animals alive and dead, alarms went off when elephants died. There had been no alarms.

Or ignore what she was told to do.

Why give her that choice? To see if she would refuse to go so he could fire her? He wasn't getting that satisfaction. What if it was for another reason – what if whatever it was that waited at those co-ordinates was dangerous?

That didn't worry her. She could deal with danger. Not knowing his motives was much more worrying.

She put the Land Rover into gear and turned back the way she had come.

Once out of sight of the inner Conservancy fence, and of Kanagi, she stopped the vehicle. She entered the co-ordinates into the satnav. They were for a ranch house a few kilometres south of the army barracks, the main training ground of the Kenyan army north of Nairobi.

If poachers were using a local ranch house, the Major would have gone there himself to claim the glory.

She knew the farm. The other rangers called it 'Barney's Brother's'. Barney ran a restaurant in town. His brother lived on that neglected ranch as he drank himself into oblivion. The rumours of how he made his money were dark. Perhaps he was the sort of man who could be involved in poaching.

Something still didn't smell right. It felt like a trap.

She put the car in gear and set off to spring it.

Jayne Farnworth is an ex-homicide detective. She is drawing on twenty-three years of experience with the Metropolitan Police to write authentic crime fiction. *Breakfast Rules* is her debut novel.

jaynefarnworth@yahoo.com

Breakfast Rules

OCTOBER 1992 – PEN Y FAN, WALES

It's twilight in the Brecon Beacons, but they don't know this; all sense of time lost in the dense fog that cloaks the mountain. Visibility is down to just a few feet and against all principles, the platoon of Army trainees and instructors has spread out over eighty metres, splintered into groups of two or three as they snake along the escarpment below the hidden summit of Pen Y Fan. They are reliant upon the lead soldier's navigation skills and the percussion of boots ahead to guide them to the next checkpoint.

From out front comes a muffled cry, a scuffle of displaced rock then silence.

'Medic. Medic! Man down, man down!'

Trained field medic, Corporal Norris, is bringing up the rear. Norris sprints towards the noise, almost colliding with a recruit. Watts is less than a foot from the edge of the ridge, peering into the impenetrable pewter mist.

Watts bends over and shouts, 'You OK, mate?' then turns to his instructor. 'He's gone off the edge, Corporal. Fucking hell. Have you got a radio?'

'No. Sergeant White and the Captain have them.'

'But they're all ahead of us.'

'Yes. Who's down there?'

'Might be Dunn, he was the last one I saw.' Watts leans further over the edge, as if six more inches will make him heard. 'Dunn? Dunny? You OK?'

There is no response.

'Watts, get on ahead, keep yelling, catch them up. We need everyone back here. I'll scramble down, take a look.'

'Jesus Christ. But Corporal, the Major said we should never split up—'

'We've no choice, Watts. Whatever state Dunn is in down there, we're going to need help getting him up. Get going. That's an order.'

'Yes, Corporal.' Recruit Watts disappears into the fog, hollering for the platoon to come back.

Norris scrambles fifteen feet below the ridge. It's not Dunn who's fallen, it's Sergeant Paul Hunt. Hunt-the-cunt. He is sprawled precariously on a narrow outcrop, conscious but dazed, in shock. His right femur has a compound fracture, the broken bone protruding through torn camouflage fabric and the hairy skin of his thigh. Blood is leaking from the wound and pooling on the sandstone beneath him. From the volume of blood gushing from his body with every heartbeat, it seems the splintered bone has grazed the wall of the femoral artery. His face is as grey and damp as the mist that surrounds them, his lips bordering on blue. Without the Corporal's medic skills, Hunt will bleed out in minutes.

Norris quickly assesses what should be done: Hunt needs a boot in his groin to stem the flow whilst a tourniquet is fastened tight around the top of his thigh, as close to the groin as possible. This will dam back the blood and see him fit for fifteen minutes, so the wound can be dressed. The rest of the platoon will return and strap him onto a makeshift stretcher. They'll release the tourniquet for thirty seconds — limiting nerve damage and oxygen deprivation to the limb — and tie it off again before a helicopter arrives to fly him off to a trauma unit. The surgeons will work swiftly: a routine wash of the wound, suturing of blood vessels, pinning of the bone. They'll pump him with morphine and antibiotics and he'll be back in action within a year.

But Norris does not move.

Hunt licks his dry, blue lips and groans.

Corporal Norris stares into the sergeant's eyes.

Hunt tries to raise his head. 'Hel, help me, p-please ... please.' The effort exhausts him and his helmet slams back against the rock.

Norris remains still for a couple more seconds, then stamps a boot onto Hunt's broken leg, aiming for the wound. With all the blood, it's a guess as to where that actually is. Still, it does the trick. Hunt lets out a howl and loses consciousness.

Finally, Norris kneels, opens the first aid kit, rips plastic to release a tourniquet, and places it exactly where it should go — but doesn't tighten it — then presses two fingers onto Hunt's carotid artery: he's still fighting, but the pulse is very weak. Norris tears sterile packaging from two large field dressings, places the pads on either side of the protruding bone and straps these around Hunt's thigh. The pad is soaked before the bandage is tied, so a second, then third layer of padding is applied. Another check of the pulse. Nothing.

Sergeant Hunt is dead.

Norris slowly nods.

In the fog above there is shouting, and the thud of boots on rock. The platoon have found their way back.

Norris pulls hard on the tourniquet and locks it off, then yells, 'Down here! Casualty critical, radio a chopper, urgent. Urgent! He's unconscious, broken femur, probably lost at least four pints. He's in a bad way.'

SEPTEMBER 1996

Hammersmith Police Station
Early Turn – Monday

Footsteps echoed in the concrete stairwell. Baxter tilted her head towards the fire escape of the empty CID office. Solid heels, brisk pace: not McCoy then, with his slothful rubber-soled shuffle. It was DI Krenis who burst through the back door in a cloud of Chanel, sunglasses perched on her head, handbag swinging from a crooked elbow.

'Morning. You must be DC Baxter? Welcome to the madhouse. Anything I should know about?' she said, striding through the cluttered corridor of desks towards her corner office.

'Er, no Ma'am. Not really.' Baxter felt a red flush creeping up her neck as she watched the elegant retreating figure of Detective Inspector Kate Krenis glide out of sight.

'It's DC Rose, actually,' she mumbled. 'Baxter's my first name.'

DI Krenis looked much friendlier in the flesh than she did in the photo on the board outside the CID office – in that portrait there was an unfortunate hint of Myra Hindley about her. Her new boss had been on holiday since Baxter had arrived. Now that she'd met her, Baxter wondered how anyone could look that immaculate and stylish so early in the morning. She sighed and looked down at her own black suit, irritated by the shiny hue of the cheap fabric.

It was 7:25am and the start of Baxter Rose's second week as a newly appointed Detective at Hammersmith Police station. She'd been first in for early turn – the day shift – and was reading the log of crimes and events written by the night duty detectives before their graveyard shift ended. She'd learnt the hard way, while scrambling her way up from uniform to plain clothes, that switched-on DCs arrived early to bag the glory crimes.

Arriving on time meant you'd cop the boring fraud jobs.

There were two prisoners in the bin that morning; neither were ripe for a weighty investigation. Baxter was scanning the list of overnight crime reports, when the DI reappeared beside her.

'Is the kettle on, Rosie?' Kate Krenis was swinging a chipped Crimewatch mug from a hooked finger.

Would anyone ever get her name right? Baxter silently cursed her father for saddling her with his mother's maiden name. She topped up the scaled old kettle with water from a plastic jug and flicked on the switch.

'So, just the two prisoners today?' Krenis turned her back to spoon instant coffee into her mug. 'What are they in for?'

'One's in for handling stolen goods, the other is just a rubbish domestic.'

The DI spun around, slate-grey eyes flashing anger.

'Don't let me catch you saying, *just a rubbish domestic*, ever again DC Baxter. Do you hear me?'

'Sorry, I didn't mean anything by it, it's just ...' Baxter's cheeks flushed crimson again; she'd been careless with her word choices.

'Yes, and that's probably what he'll say when you ask him why his wife has a swollen lip, or a broken rib, or worse. I will not have domestic violence offences treated with contempt.'

'Sorry Ma'am. It's just frustrating sometimes when women end up refusing to press charges.'

'If a victim withdraws a complaint, that means you have to try harder. You give her your phone number – *just* your number mind, no name and rank for him to find – and you tell her to call you anytime. Eventually, you'll be at your desk and she *will* call you, and hopefully not from A&E.'

Krenis over-poured hot water into her mug, and Baxter watched the coffee dribble down the *Crimewatch* logo, adding to the stains on top of the office fridge.

'I'm sorry, Ma'am, I didn't intend to come across as dismissive. I honestly do understand.' Baxter was struggling to hold eye contact with her new boss. 'I'm just keen to pick up a case I can really get my teeth into.'

Krenis took a sip of coffee, before heading for the main door. She gave Baxter an appraising glance.

'Be careful what you wish for, DC Baxter.'

'It's Rose, actually, Ma'am.'

'Not when I'm giving you advice it isn't, DC Baxter,' said Krenis, not looking back. 'And stop calling me Ma'am, I'm not the bloody Queen Mother.'

It was 3:00pm. After charging her prisoner for selling stolen PlayStations, Baxter returned to the CID office to find it buzzing with laughter and conversations. Two male DCs were teasing a female colleague about her new highlights and the late turn team were chatting to a couple of uniforms. Baxter exchanged nods with everyone as she passed but realised she still didn't know most of her new workmates.

She'd certainly got the measure of her immediate supervisor, though. DS Dennis McCoy was a work-shy Scouser with a corned beef complexion and a predilection for vodka and nurses – both of which she suspected he'd indulged in during his late shifts with Baxter. McCoy was sitting in a fog of cigarette smoke inspecting a pile of pornographic videos on his ash-strewn desk. He looked up as she sank into her chair.

'Get the coffees in, will you?'

Baxter chose not to answer.

He held out an unboxed video cassette. 'Here, you'll like this one, it's a classic: Assablanca? No? OK, what about Forrest Hump?'

McCoy gave a throaty laugh and heaved his lumpy body out of his chair, revealing a torn cushion with a sizable indentation. 'Oi, Dave! I've got a Debbie Does Dallas here. Pint of Guinness and it's yours pal.'

He was unbearable. After removing the Twix and Mars Bar wrappers that he'd discarded on her desk, Baxter began assembling a court file for the handling job. McCoy put on his coat and filled his pockets with a lighter, two packs of Marlboro Reds and a rectangular-shaped package wrapped in a Tesco carrier bag.

'Right,' he said, 'I'm off on enquiries.'

'Oh, has a job come in?'

'Nothing for you to worry about, girlie.'

So, just skiving off early then.

Baxter held out her file. 'Before you go, Dennis, would you mind signing off my case summary, please?'

He looked at her like she'd asked him to donate an organ. 'Can't you get someone else to do it? In fact, no, just print my name and do a squiggle. And bag up those videos, will you, then take them to the property office. Can't trust any of these dirty bastards.'

Before she could protest, McCoy had shuffled over to the fire escape, slamming the door behind him. Baxter sighed heavily and began threading a treasury tag through the case papers.

'DC Baxter?'

Baxter looked across the room to see DI Krenis at the open doorway of her office, leaning, arms folded against the door frame. Baxter wondered how long she'd been there, and if she'd noticed her pulling the knicker seam out of her bum.

'Give me five minutes, then pop in and see me, will you?' She turned away, not waiting for an answer.

'OK, boss.'

Baxter jumped up and made for the ladies. After their conversation earlier that morning, she needed to make a better impression. Standing in front of a cracked full-length mirror in the toilet that doubled as a locker room, she frowned. First off, her suit trousers were creased in all the wrong places, and the hem on the right leg was trailing on the floor — the brown packing tape she'd used in a failed attempt at repair was clearly visible and flecked with debris. Her tatty black loafers had mud caked into the seams after an earlier crime scene visit, and the right toe was splashed with something sticky. Her white shirt was tinged with pink from a red t-shirt that had strayed into the white load and beneath her jacket lapels, the collar was crumpled and flaccid.

You're a mess, girl. Get a grip, for God's sake.

She snatched a wad of green paper towels, briefly held them under a tap, and then scrubbed the worst of the mud from her shoes. She tore the filthy tape from her hem, washed her hands and raked wet fingers through her red curls, trying to encourage some symmetry. Finally, she buttoned her jacket to conceal the blushing blouse, and pulled her collar to attention. Slightly better.

Baxter made her way back into the main office, took a deep breath and knocked on the boss's open door.

'Sit down, Rosie.' She nodded at the low armchair in front of her desk. 'I'll be two seconds – just need to finish this.'

Krenis turned to face her computer and began typing. Baxter sank awkwardly into the chair. Krenis now towered above her. This was clearly a tactic, placing her staff in a submissive position – admirable for a five-and-a-half-foot woman in a job over-populated with tall men. Trying to raise her posture, Baxter edged forward to perch on the front of the seat and accidentally kicked the DI's handbag. She watched in horror as it toppled over, releasing a super-sized tampon that rolled across the floor, through the open door into the main office. Bending over, Baxter righted the bag, then glanced sideways at an oblivious Krenis. The Tampax could wait.

The DI's perfect scarlet nails deftly stroked the keys, her expert touch-typing allowing full focus on the screen. There was no wedding band, just a weighty crested gold signet ring on her left pinky finger, which occasionally knocked against the shift key.

'Right, done.' Krenis swivelled her chair and almost smiled. 'How are you getting on, Rosie?'

'Fine. Thanks. It's Baxter actually.' She was flustered again. Krenis was casting her eyes up and down Baxter's suit. She uncrossed her legs. 'Yes, you know, still finding my feet, you know ... getting used to the team ... but, yes.'

'Good. Talking of team, where's Dennis?'

Baxter hesitated, then said, 'He's out on enquiries.'

Krenis leaned forward across the desk, arching her eyebrows above her tortoiseshell glasses.

'Really?' She pushed back into her chair, clearly not convinced. Pausing for a beat, she moved on. 'You missed the CID office meeting earlier, you'd been sent out to a robbery, hadn't you?'

'Yes, another one in Ravenscourt Park.'

'Any leads?'

Baxter shook her head.

'I'm making this spate of robberies a priority, that's one of the things we talked about in the meeting. The main discussion point was staffing. I'm restructuring the teams, Rosie. You'll be staying with Dennis McCoy. There'll also be a uniform joining you on a temporary attachment – Superintendent Patmore's new project, breaking down the barriers and all that. I haven't decided who I'm taking yet. And, I'm moving Neil Sharpe to your team too.'

Baxter tried not to react. Neil Sharpe was a total prat from what she'd seen. Great. Two idiots now.

'He's been in court since last week,' Krenis continued, 'so, you might not have met him. Tall, slim, dark hair.'

'I think I've seen him around.' Usually hovering beside WPCs or chatting up the canteen ladies.

'Anyway, you'll be partnering up with Neil. Starting tomorrow. That's all.'

AL

That first time, I felt dead proud. I was buzzing, knowing I'd done something for a mate, for a good cause, no harm done. Well, there wasn't really, not physical harm anyway. We'd done it for Hannah, not that she knew about it. Still doesn't. It was after a night in the pub, when she'd had way too many vodkas and told us all how the speed-date bloke had treated her. She was in pieces, sobbing her heart out, said he'd got her blind drunk, taken advantage and then afterwards totally blanked her, made her feel cheap. Basically, been a bastard. Hannah said she felt humiliated. I decided me and Frankie ought to give him a scare, teach him a lesson. Chicken-shit Frankie took some convincing, but I can be very persuasive when I need to be. We agreed to do it the next night.

We knew where he lived because Hannah had let slip it was above the bike shop, with a metal fire escape at the back. That was how she got out of the flat after she'd been woken up by that wanker and told to leave. At 3am, in the dark, pissed. Bastard. Hannah told us he was assistant manager at the bingo hall, so I just put in a call and asked to speak to him. Whoever answered said, *He's in the office, I'll get him for you,* so I put the phone down and said to Frankie, *It's a go, go, go,* and up the fire escape we went. I'd grabbed an old tea towel and I told Frankie to nab half a brick from a skip we passed in the side street. I put the towel against one of the squares of glass in the panelled door and then slammed the brick into it. The glass cracked so quietly. Made me look like a fucking pro. We were inside in less than a minute.

Frankie was fucking useless, of course. Being a liability, all on edge and twitching. I can't be doing with lack of commitment. I had to have words.

The plan was simply to give the bastard a fright, put the wind up him. Make a bit of a mess, leave him a couple of messages. We wrote all over his walls, things like, *you're dead, wanker, watch your back.* After that, I went through the flat trashing everything, you know, pulling food from the fridge, emptying drawers, throwing his CDs off the racks – fucking Boyzone fan – I kid you not. I stamped on that one. Just as we were about to scarper, I had an idea. I ripped open a bag of frozen prawns I'd tugged out of the freezer, stuffed them in a football sock and slipped it under his mattress. Figured that'd screw up his shagging career for a while. It made Frankie crack a smile anyway.

Hammersmith Police Station
Early Turn – Tuesday

When Baxter parked her bike in the yard at the back of the nick, she was soaking wet, and she stank. The wind and rain were brutal that morning, but nowhere near as brutal as the skip lorry that had cut her up in King Street, causing a pedal to catch the kerb and resulting in her sliding into a pile of leaking bin bags. Stiff, smelly and drenched, she walked slowly up the back steps to the CID office feeling like she'd cheated death.

It was 7:25am. Neil Sharpe had his head in the fridge.

'Hiya,' he said, head still level with the wire racks. 'I put a sausage sandwich in here on Friday and some bugger's had it.'

He pushed the door closed and stood up, thrusting out a huge right hand for Baxter to shake.

'Neil Sharpe,' he said, 'But you can call me Lord.' He laughed. 'Nah, just kidding, everyone calls me Sharpey. Probably because they've got no imagination.'

Baxter looked at him blankly. Rain was dripping from her hair. She held out her blood-smeared right hand. They both stared down at it. Baxter dropped it to her side, and then offered her left hand, which was clarted with mud. At least she hoped it was mud. She pulled it away a millisecond before Sharpey clasped it.

'Christ, do you normally look this rough first thing, Rosie?'

'I'm going for a shower.' Baxter made for the stairs. 'My name's Baxter. Baxter Rose. Why the hell can no one get it right?'

Fifteen minutes later Baxter returned to the office to find a steaming cup of tea on her desk. Not a bad brew, actually. Sharpey had disappeared and McCoy was yet to arrive. No change there then. The main office door opened and in walked one of the uniforms: slim, blonde, hair cut just short enough to get away with not tying it in a bun, inappropriate red lipstick. She tottered towards Baxter, grinning inanely.

'Hi-yah, do you know where Sharpey is?'

'No idea, sorry.'

'Oh well, I'll just leave this here for him, then. Tell him Gemma came up, will you.'

Gemma carefully placed a jam doughnut on top of Sharpey's clipboard, then left. She'd been gone less than a minute when the main door opened again. A pretty black girl popped her head around the door, saw Baxter, and said, 'Oh hello, just looking for Sharpey. Do you know—'

Baxter shook her head, 'No idea.'

The office door opened once more. Baxter looked up and saw it was another female officer.

'He's not here,' she clipped.

The girl was approaching the row of desks. 'Are you DC Baxter?'

Here we go. Baxter sighed. 'No, I'm DC *Rose*.'

'Oh. The Control Room said DC Baxter was early turn.'

'I'm early turn. My name's Baxter Rose. DC Baxter Rose. And I wish I had a pound for every time I've said that. What's up?'

'God, that must get annoying. It's sort of back to front though, isn't it? I'm Nisha, by the way, nice to meet you. Oh hello, Sharpey,'

Sharpey sauntered over to join them. 'All right, Nish?'

'Just a heads up,' said Nisha. 'A MISPER: Keith Moxon. Not been at work for four days, not called in sick, not answering the phone. His car's parked up. Wife walked out on him recently and he's on anti-depressants. Brother called it in, worried he might have topped himself. He's travelled up from Bristol and he's at the house now but doesn't have keys. 9 Claxton Grove.'

'Yep, know it,' said Sharpey, 'road next to the cemetery, near my favourite greasy spoon. We'll head down there, Nisha.'

'Nice one, Sharpey, I'll tell the Control Room.'

Baxter waited until Nisha had left the office, then turned to Sharpey. 'Why are you volunteering us for a call that a lid should take?'

'I wouldn't usually, but there are no prisoners and I was going to take you out for a coffee. It's a win, win, we appear helpful by freeing up a uniform – and believe me, I need to get back on the Duty Officer's good side – the call's likely to be nothing, and then we've got an excuse for going to Maggie's caff.'

'Yeah, OK, but don't make a habit of it. I left my uniform behind for a reason.' Baxter picked up the CID car keys. 'We'd better check there's a big red key in the boot.'

'Good point: no house keys. We'll definitely need the enforcer.'

What was left of the door hung on bruised hinges above a carpet of junk mail. Probably two days' worth, Baxter reckoned. Behind her, Sharpey lay the enforcer on the doorstep. There was something written on the hallway mirror. That was the first thing Baxter noticed as they stepped through the splintered door frame into the dimly-lit entrance.

Keith Moxon's brother hovered on the threshold. 'The alarm's not on,' he said, biting his upper lip, 'it usually beeps as soon as the door opens.

He always sets the alarm. Even if he just pops out for a paper.'

Baxter turned around. 'Would you mind staying outside please, love?' she said, not giving him the option to mind at all, steering him back onto the garden path. 'Best wait in your car, it's brass monkeys out there this morning.' She closed the door, then tilted her head in line with the angled words on the mirror.

'What does that say, Sharpey?' She read out the words as she deciphered the large, cursive handwriting. 'I can make out *Bid. Joy. For. N?* Is that right?'

'Christ, did Yoda write it?' He looked at the mirror. *'For Bid n Joy,* is my guess. Forbidden joy?'

'The spelling is bad, but yes. Weird. Right, shall we get cracking?'

'Yeah, for what it's worth,' said Sharpey. 'Probably a waste of time. I bet he got a Teletext bargain holiday and nipped over to the Costa del Crime.' He loosened his tie. 'Talking of which, it's tropical in here, his heating bill's gonna be huge when he gets back. Let's get this over with to satisfy his brother, then we can get some scoff.'

'I'll do the upstairs,' she said. 'By the way, who's Yoda?'

Sharpey moved off down the hallway. 'I can see you'll need some *Star Wars* tuition, Baxter, if we're going to get along. God, it really stinks in here.'

Baxter began to climb the stairs. This was always the worst part. The not knowing what you're going to find bit. She sniffed instinctively, almost in time with her steps. Sharpey was right, there was an overwhelming smell of babies' nappies and rotting food hanging in the air and she regretted not having a jar of Vicks in her pocket. She paused near the top step.

'Something's not right about this place, Sharpey. The smell's worse up here. I think you'd better come up.'

Baxter snapped on latex gloves as she reached the landing and opened the first door she came to. An army of angry bluebottles engulfed her head. She cried out and began blowing and spitting as the flies sought out the moisture in her mouth and nose. Frantically brushing her cheeks, she tried to dislodge the mass of tiny legs that crawled on her face and shook her head in a vain attempt to evict those hopping amongst the curls of her hair. She slammed the door, bumping into Sharpey, now behind her on the landing.

'What the ...' he steadied her, batting away the escapee flies.

'Oh, my God, this is so gross, get them off me, Sharpey!'

'Calm down mate, most of them have gone now.' He swept half a dozen of the shiny black bodies from her shoulders. A couple remained settled in her hair. 'You know we've got to go back in there.'

'We should just call it in, he's obviously dead, or there wouldn't be bloody flies.' She shook out her curls, expelling the last of the buzzing insects.

'Baxter, we can't call it in until we know what we've got. It might be a week's worth of take-out curry cartons and KFC bones that we can smell. Flies don't always mean death.'

'I know, I know ... it's just. Disgusting.'

Keith Moxon's naked body lay face up on the double bed. He was starfished: his hands and feet bound with ties and cables to the four corners of the metal bed-frame. His lower body and the sheet below him were soiled; he'd long since lost control of his bowels. Flies hopped over the fetid brown matter and buzzed around the blood-soaked hair of Moxon's groin.

Baxter was rooted to a spot on the carpet, momentarily dazed, as she scanned the room. She waved a couple of flies away. 'Poor bastard, what a way to go.'

Sharpey had a hand clamped over his nose and made an incomprehensible sound she assumed was agreement.

Around the bed, four black plastic bin bags had been torn and emptied of their contents. The floor was strewn with rotting food, cartons, cans and paper. Tiny maggots were feasting on the food debris and insects crawled on almost every surface.

She glanced at her partner. His face was pale and filmed with sweat.

'Sharpey, do you need to go out and get some—'

Sharpey heaved and ran from the room, vomit dripping from his hands. She heard him expel the contents of his stomach and hoped it wasn't on top of any evidence.

She turned her attention back to Keith Moxon and retched. Bile burned the back of her throat, but despite her revulsion, she knew she had to take in every detail, embed it into her memory. She swallowed, tried not to breathe, and moved closer to the bed.

There was a wound in his upper right thigh, close to his groin, likely caused by a knife. Moxon's head was wrapped in cling film, several layers by the look of it, like a joint of sirloin ready for the freezer. His eyes were open beneath the transparent mummification, eyelashes crushed against the plastic. Around his mouth the cling film was fogged and wet with condensation. Baxter leaned in closer and noticed small slits in the wrapping under the nose. His head moved. She jumped back.

'He's alive! Oh, my God, Sharpey, he's alive.'

Natasha Hutcheson has worked in museums, archaeology and heritage for 25 years. She studied archaeology at UCL and later gained a PhD from UEA. Her interest in the interplay between the past and present has shaped her approach to writing crime fiction. *Silenced Revelations* is her debut novel.

Natasha@najla19.plus.com

Silenced Revelations

CHAPTER ONE

Sasha watched the three people sitting across from her wince in unison. The scream from a child two tables down was ear-splitting. She gave an apologetic smile, regretting her suggestion they meet in the hollow space of the museum's café. It was unusually busy for a Tuesday afternoon in early January. The New Year had come in on a blast of chilled air, and the cold, coupled with the last day of the school Christmas break, was driving restless young families out of their houses and to indoor distractions.

The man, Joshua – not Josh – sported a long, well-manicured beard. He was talking with animation, his words coming fast, cutting through the insistent wailings that ricocheted off the café's ageing walls. Dana and Lizzie, his business partners, sat either side of him.

Despite Joshua's obvious excitement, Sasha was struggling to concentrate. The noise wasn't helping, but mostly it was nerves interfering with her hearing; this was the first commission that had come in for the museum's newly established Historic Research Service, and Joshua, Dana and Lizzie were her first clients. She took a swig of espresso and furrowed her brow, attempting again to focus on what he was saying.

'That's why we're opening a café-cum-deli,' he concluded. 'On Elm Hill. Do you know it?'

His eyes were expectant.

She nodded. Of course she knew it. Norwich was a small city, not much above a mile from north to south as the crow flies, within the medieval walls at least. A mish-mash of cobbles and Tudor buildings, Elm Hill had not escaped her notice.

'It's so historic,' he went on. 'And so cheap compared to London. I know I shouldn't keep saying it, but really, Norwich is such an investment opportunity for us right now. Such a great place to open a new business.'

He wasn't wrong. In the five years since Sasha had made Norwich her home, the city had changed. House prices had sky-rocketed and it seemed new cafés were opening everywhere. A church for each week of the year and a pub for each day was how it had been known, and although pubs were still plentiful, a vibrant café society was beginning to redefine the old city.

'So, the deli-café is on Elm Hill,' he said again, 'and we're going vegan. No dairy, you know. None whatsoever.'

Dana and Lizzie nodded in agreement. In Sasha's opinion, soya milk ruined a good coffee, but knowing her tastes to be old-fashioned, she smiled in acquiescence at the trio.

She opened her laptop and, with a flutter of excitement, looked at the blank Initial Consultation form created several weeks earlier. It had taken some time to convince John Sloucher, the Museum Director, that the Historic Research Service was a good idea. And although it had been given the green light, he'd made it clear she was on her own with this one. It was down to her to make it work – on top of her day job as the museum's Senior Curator.

'It all sounds great, a new café.' Sasha tucked a disorderly strand of dark hair behind her ear. 'But, what can I do to help?'

Joshua took hold of Lizzie and Dana's hands. Their manicured nails wrapped round his palms as he lifted them to the table. He smiled at the women in turn, and then, as if he was announcing they were all expecting a child together, turned to Sasha.

'We are going to call our café "Emily's".'

His face suggested this was enough information, that it explained their presence. Sasha frowned again, struggling to see the role of the Historic Research Service in their new venture. She was pleased when one of the women filled the gap with a tinkling, almost mechanical sounding laugh.

'Joshua,' said Dana, 'I think we need to give Dr Miles a little more to go on.'

As she spoke, she leaned forward and produced a wooden box from an expensive-looking leather tote and placed it on the table.

'We found this,' she said. 'Under a floorboard on the first floor.'

The box was decorated with a delicate vine-like pattern fashioned from different shades of inlaid wood. It was rectangular, around the size of a small shoe box. A diamond of mother-of-pearl surrounded a tiny lock. It was a beautiful thing, Sasha could see that, probably mid-nineteenth century.

'May I?' She reached to pick the box up.

The three new café owners nodded as one.

'We think it's a jewellery box,' said Lizzie, speaking for the first time. She drew a petite, brass key from the pocket of her jeans and handed it to Sasha.

'Would you like to open it?' she asked.

Sasha turned the lock. Inside, the box was quite plain. It was lined with a creamy coloured silk, disintegrating into the corners. A tray sat in the top of the box, split into five compartments; four small ones in one half, and a larger one in the other. She removed a pair of cotton gloves from her pocket and pulled them on, then gently pressed a finger into one of the small compartments. The padding beneath the silk gave in response to the pressure, still soft and ready to protect its contents.

Another of the compartments had a circular depression.

'I think a ring must have lain here for a long time,' said Sasha.

'That's what I thought,' said Lizzie, leaning forward.

Sasha continued. 'Each of these compartments would have held various trinkets over the years, and below the tray, there should be a space for larger items. May I?' she asked, carefully pulling at a loop attached to the central partition. The trio nodded again, and the tray came free.

Sasha was not usually one for bothering with conservation protocol, but on this occasion, she was pleased she'd used the cotton gloves. Beneath the tray lay a sheet of folded paper, cream like the silk interior. She removed the paper and carefully unfolded it. It was a letter. The handwriting was exquisite. And despite its obvious age, the ink was as clear as it must have been the day the letter was written.

Three pairs of eyes were on her as she read the note.

Emily Myhill, 4th August, 1863
erstwhile of Elm Hill, Norwich

To my dearest Eliza,

 I feel that despite my best efforts, Canon Foulger has blackened my name and likened my defence to the 'blasphemous and senseless tittle-tattle of a hysterical gossip'. Both you and I know whence this came and what it must mean. I meant for nothing to happen to our darling John, and though I know you may never read this note, I feel I must write it and be clear in my own mind that I am innocent. And that John is innocent. We are both innocent except perhaps in loving and helping one another in a most honest fashion. But we have met with darker forces than I could imagine, and like your sweetest brother, I am now to be silenced.

Until forever, Your Loving
Emily

'That's why we are calling the café "Emily's",' said Joshua, a wide grin on his face. 'She must have lived on Elm Hill, in our building. We want you to find out her history, if you can.'

Sasha folded the letter and placed it back in the box. Anticipation trickled through her veins.

'We've done a bit of research,' continued Joshua, 'but haven't come across much. We got a history on Elm Hill and found some old pictures that show our building. But not so much on Emily.'

Dana reached into her bag.

'I've done a bit of googling and printed this out,' she said, placing a sheet of paper onto the table. The print was fuzzy, cut and pasted from an old news-sheet. Sasha scanned the image and noted it was from the front page of the *Norwich Mercury*, dated 29th August, 1863.

'Look at this.' Dana pointed to a small notice she'd highlighted in lurid green. 'Emily Myhill was hanged. In public. Here, at the castle prison in Norwich.'

'And according to her note,' chimed in Lizzie, 'she was innocent'.

'Can you find out more?' asked Joshua. 'Why she was hanged, and whether she was actually innocent? Other than a couple of small newspaper notices, we couldn't find any more about her.'

'We want to put the box and letter on display,' said Lizzie, 'you know, bring her back to life. It would be great, would really make our café stand out, attract the customers.'

Sasha nodded. She could try. That was the aim of the HRS, sharing history, at one level anyway. Making some money for the museum was another consideration.

She took a sip of coffee. A hanging was definitely good for her first commission, even if it hadn't been quite so lucky for Emily Myhill. There should be a paper trail. The museum had been the county gaol for over seven hundred years and the city's prison records were still fairly intact within the museum's own archives, so she had resources at her fingertips. Whether she could prove or disprove innocence was another matter.

She ran her finger over the mouse pad of her laptop, conscious that if the woman had been hanged, at some point she would have walked through the room they now sat in; a room scented with the acrid smell of candle-wax, soot and fear, rather than sweet pastries and coffee. Her screen sprang to life and she looked once more at the expectant faces opposite.

Writing a number 'one' into the job-number box at the top of the form, Sasha sent up a silent thank you to Emily Myhill. The Historic Research Service was officially trading.

CHAPTER TWO

It was nearly midday. Francesca stood in front of the light brown door. Modern and heavy, it was at odds with the uneven flint and limestone walls that defined the cathedral. The door hid a flight of steps to the library, separating them from the visitors and worshippers milling in the cathedral's hostry. She could see her reflection in the small, toughened glass panel, an almost invisible chequerboard of mesh securing her shadowy face behind bars. She shuddered.

A confident set of footsteps caught her attention. The Dean, walking too close to the young woman at his side, was coming from the main body of the church. A gust of cold January air filled the space. She pushed at the door, passed to the other side and pressed her back against the wall, heart thumping. The coolness of the stone slid into her body and she chided herself for being ridiculous.

She'd done nothing wrong.

It was the mantra she'd kept in her head since yesterday evening. The cathedral had a library and she'd borrowed some items. *That was all.*

Not stolen.

Just borrowed.

She breathed deeply and made her way up the steps, bracing herself as she got closer to the library.

'Francesca. I thought I heard you arrive. Have you been at the museum this morning?'

Daniel Carcelli appeared in the doorway of the library's built-in cupboard-cum-kitchen. His tall, solid body filled the frame, and light caught his red-brown hair, thick and wavy, from behind.

'I had to pop in. To see Sasha. Exhibition stuff.' Francesca was impressed she'd kept her voice even. She hung her coat next to Daniel's, green wool next to black, and carried on, concentrating on sounding casual.

'Is Father Kenneth in yet?' she asked.

The Canon Librarian's desk sat at the top of the library, the high altar, overlooking a study area and rows of book-laden shelves beyond. It was empty.

'He's around, was in earlier,' said Daniel. 'Went off to a meeting, I think. I'll grab you a coffee.'

Francesca exhaled and tightened the belt of her cardigan. Her heart missed a beat. It was possible, probable even, that Father Kenneth had read her email by now, must know what she'd done.

Daniel disappeared into the kitchen. Turning, she made her way to a substantial wooden table that stood along the wall of the study area, her sensible, soft-soled shoes silent on the thick red carpet. Three work stations were set up; one for her, one for Daniel, Library Manager and Father Kenneth's assistant, and one for Sophie, a young volunteer who'd been working on the *Medieval Manuscripts of Norwich* exhibition project with them for the last six months.

She settled herself at the central workstation and pulled a large notebook from her bag. It overflowed with bits of paper and images, fragments of ideas gathered and ready for weaving into the imminent exhibition. A stylised, medieval angel shimmered on its cover – exhibition appropriate.

Drawing on a pair of white cotton gloves, Francesca flicked on the computer in front of her and opened one of the last box files of medieval folios waiting to be catalogued. Reaching in, she removed an old document, a vellum folio; goatskin paper folded in half, creating four leaves all adorned with the writings of a medieval scribe.

The familiarity of cataloguing gave her confidence. She reflected again on the escapade of the previous evening; was sure she'd done the right thing. A smile played at her lips. In only a few weeks, she would be responsible for bringing to light the most important manuscripts ever written in Norwich. It was exhilarating.

'Here you go.' Daniel placed a lidded mug on the mat in front of her, making her jump. She pulled her hand away from the document, aware of her fingers grazing his as she did. She felt her face flush. He sat beside her.

'I hope you're still up for lunch today,' he said. 'The next few weeks will be crazy. We deserve a treat before the madness starts.'

She nodded. Her mind floated momentarily to its regular daydream: *Francesca Carcelli*. Maybe she could switch from ugly duckling to swan, from buttoned-up English museum curator to free-spirited Italian lover. Not that Daniel had any trace of an Italian accent, she just assumed he was Italian because of his surname. She pushed her straight blonde fringe away from her eyes and wondered what he would make of her daring; then felt the familiar rush of heat spread across her cheeks again.

'Is Sophie coming to lunch too?' she asked, hoping the blush was not too obvious.

'No.' Daniel smiled. 'She's not in until this afternoon, an extra shift at her job, I think.'

—

Dreaming of lunch with Daniel Carcelli and actually having lunch with him were proving to be two different things, Francesca was discovering.

She sat in a dimly-lit booth in the basement of the Dandelion Clock café. The gloomy, low-ceilinged space was hung with fairy lights and filled with mismatched furniture. Tumbling spider plants and candle holders, thick with hardened rivulets of wax, adorned an old mantelpiece; bric-a-brac and old tat. The dull light of mid-winter barely broke through from the single window, ceiling height and narrow.

She rubbed her hands together. The whole place felt grubby, not what she'd envisaged at all. A sandwich or bowl of soup in the cathedral's new refectory, somewhere open and safe, full of people more like her was what she'd expected. The Dandelion Clock was too hippy or trendy, or something. She didn't really have the right language to describe it.

She tightened her cardigan in an attempt to keep out the cool damp air the open fire was failing to combat. Daniel ordered their lunch at the improvised bar. Despite his vestments and small silver cross, he seemed somehow to fit in. He returned to the table, a tray balanced with china cups and saucers and two ornate, tea-stained pots in his hands.

'You know, Francesca,' he said, pouring a weak cup of camomile tea for her. 'Ever since we started this project, the one thing I hoped we might find buried in the archive are the original Mother Julian Manuscripts. We've uncovered so many medieval gems in the collection, but not them.'

Heat crept up her neck once more. This line of conversation was completely unexpected, he'd never mentioned the Julian manuscripts before. Not the originals. She said nothing.

'It's great the British Library are lending the Amherst copy, and the Sloane version. They'll really make the exhibition. But do you ever wonder about the originals?'

She picked up a chipped cup, the sight of its pale yellow, slightly gritty liquid turning her stomach. It burned her lips and tongue as she sipped. She put the cup down again, hands shaking. She couldn't speak. The image of the original manuscripts nestling in her bag less than two hours earlier flitted through her mind.

A waitress carrying two plates glided towards their table, catching Daniel's attention. Young and slim, the waitress smiled as she placed a sandwich replete with a soggy looking garnish and a few crisps in front of Francesca. Francesca picked at a drooping slice of cucumber and watched Daniel take a bite of the ham sandwich he'd ordered. She wasn't feeling very hungry and was relieved when he started talking again.

'It is possible the manuscripts were destroyed when Henry VIII dissolved the monasteries. But, if they survived, they might have gone over to France. There was that group of nuns exiled from the Abbey at Carrow. Early 17th century if I remember rightly. What do you think?'

An awkward silence descended between them. She nodded, eyes on her plate. The noise in the rest of the small room seem to increase. She knew neither scenario was true; but also knew that his research was impeccable.

She picked at a crisp. A copy of the manuscripts had certainly ended up in France, where it was undoubtedly copied again until first published by Serenus de Cressy. But the originals, those written in Mother Julian's hand had gone nowhere. Her heart throbbed in her ears, and she hauled in a breath. She was going to tell him. They could share the surprise, share the glory.

A group of young people, red-nosed and clothed in jeans, furry boots and thick coats tumbled into the basement room, the scent of chilled air descending with them. Daniel took another bite of his sandwich and turned his head at the noise. Francesca put down the crisp and opened her mouth to speak.

'They're not lost. Mother Julian's manuscripts. They're still here.'

She'd whispered, but it was loud enough. Daniel turned back to face her, swallowed his mouthful and put his sandwich down. She stared at her plate again, felt her cheeks pale. Something between panic and excitement thrummed through her.

'What do you mean, they're still here?'

'They're here. In Norwich.' It felt powerful knowing; she felt powerful.

'Have you seen them?' His face was incredulous. 'Have you seen them, touched the work of Mother Julian? Here in the cathedral?'

She looked up and nodded, relaxed. Her heart rate slowed; a sense of equilibrium was returning. It was OK what she'd done. It was the right thing to do. She could feel it now she'd shared the secret with Daniel. Father Kenneth could be dealt with later.

'Hey Daniel.' A voice called across the basement. They turned to see a young man lope across the room, weaving between the uneven chairs and tables and skirting a threadbare sofa, his loose-fitting coat almost catching a gaudy, green and blue jug.

'Good to see you, man,' the young man patted Daniel's shoulder and pulled up a stool too short to accommodate his long legs. Daniel leaned back in his chair and smiled.

'Ha, Jack. Good to see you too. What are you doing in here?'

Jack ignored the question and turned to Francesca.

'He's my saviour, this one,' he said. 'Thanks to him, I don't spend all day in bed and all night on the booze. Made me join me pub's footy team, picks me up every Sunday and makes me play. Even got me a job in an old antiques shop. More of a flea market really.'

Francesca nodded.

'All I did was give you a tiny nudge, Jack,' said Daniel. 'The rest was down to you.'

Francesca hadn't considered Daniel's religion before, not properly. He'd never mentioned his ministry outside of the library and she'd focused solely on his role as custodian, and his probable Italian roots.

'It was mostly you, Daniel,' said Jack, 'but thanks. And I'm studying now, aren't I?' He turned to Francesca. 'I hope to become a man of the cloth too.'

Francesca managed to swallow her mouthful of tea, getting it down before spraying it across the table; he looked an unlikely future vicar with his skinny black jeans, tired Converse and a washed-out Lemonheads T-shirt. Daniel intervened.

'You're giving the game away now, Jack,' he said. 'Making it sound like I'm out converting footballers and drinkers into vicars wherever I go.'

'Oh yeah, sorry mate.' Jack winked. 'She not part of your flock?'

Daniel smiled at her.

'No, no. Francesca is a colleague. A professional historian, curator at the museum. She's been working on some old manuscripts with me. That exhibition I was telling you about.'

Jack nodded. 'If you like old stuff,' he said, 'you'll have to pop into the shop sometime.'

Francesca smiled.

'I think Francesca has her fill of old stuff at work, Jack,' said Daniel. 'She might not want to spend her time off rummaging around flea markets.'

Jack reddened. Daniel looked at his watch and stood up.

'I'm afraid I'm going to have to get off, I have a meeting.' He turned his attention to Francesca. 'We'll talk again later.' A smile crinkled the corners of his eyes. She was looking forward to it.

Watching him go, Francesca gathered her own things and pulled on her coat. She said goodbye to Jack and made her way up the stairs and out into the cold air.

—

The world was greyer than when she'd entered the café, as if someone had turned the contrast down a notch or two on an old black-and-white film. The stone-slabbed pavements, flint walls of surrounding buildings, and damp cobbles that lined St Benedict's Street all exuded their own, individual shade, each a unique take on the sky above.

Snow threatened; she could almost smell it. She dug her hands into her coat pockets and braced herself against the cold. Without thinking, Francesca headed towards St Julian's Church, head spinning with the conversation she'd had with Daniel. She'd fill him in on the rest when she saw him later.

With reverence, she stood outside the little church. It was one of the less imposing in the city, tucked along a small alley off King Street just beyond the river, an amalgam of old and new, a hasty recovery from a WWII bomb. Frost still clung to its roof tiles, another layer of grey in the low light.

Inside St Julian's the nave was quiet, two people sat apart, contemplating in silence. Visiting the church in recent months, she'd noticed it was never empty.

She stepped into the reconstruction of Mother Julian's cell; a small room, furnished simply with a plain altar and an image of Christ. Its lime-washed walls gave the low winter sun an iridescent quality, making the cell somehow brighter than the rest of the church.

Francesca could almost feel the old nun's presence, dispensing her ministry from one window, and receiving communion through the other; a small opening between her and the nave – her and the male clergy. She glanced round and wondered again which corner Mother Julian had sat to write her *Revelations of Divine Love*, and how often her maid would have replenished her bottles of ink.

Footsteps tapped across the tiled floor of the main church; another visitor. Francesca ignored them, looked round the cell once more, and was enthralled. She would be putting Mother Julian's original works on display for the first time ever.

Saint Julian in her own words.

Not the words of a scribe and copyist, not a censored version deemed appropriate by an editor, or the church. Just her words, reaching out from the 14th century as it bled into the 15th. Press coverage for the exhibition would be phenomenal.

The footsteps did not stop in the nave, but came into the cell, resting behind her. She couldn't ignore them and turned. It was Jack. She stepped back, away from him. Why had he followed her? Her mouth went dry.

He started to speak. 'I'm so sorry, Francesca.' His voice was less assured than it had been in the café. 'I just wanted to ...'

He stopped. Clammed up. She noticed he looked much younger than she'd first thought, 21? Maybe 22? He ran long, shaky and pale fingers through his unkempt dark hair. There was an uneasiness about him, something was wrong. She moved to pass, didn't want to get involved. Didn't want him to impinge on her excitement.

Eyes on her, he stayed in the doorway, resolute, blocking her way out of the cell.

Her nerves tightened.

'Can I help?' she asked.

He opened his mouth to speak again. Then seemed to think better of it, to cave in.

'Nah, I'm fine,' he mumbled, rubbed his hand over his face and moved to one side, giving her space to pass.

Relieved, she stepped forward, was keen to get out, return to the cathedral library for the afternoon.

He moved back again, suddenly, obstructive. She stopped, her heart was beating, panic rising.

'Can you let me pass, please?'

Jack said nothing, reached into his pocket, eyes darting around. She didn't like it.

He spoke, urgency tremoring his voice.

'I wanted to give you this.'

He pulled a cream-coloured object from his pocket, a cross.

'I found it,' he said. 'In the antique shop. You know. The one I work in. I don't think it should be for sale.'

Jack's face was pale, dark skin round his eyes. He thrust the cross into her hand, hesitated briefly and then turned, heading back into the nave and hurrying out of the church. His ill-fitting coat billowed as he went.

Francesca stood for a moment, composed herself. One of the worshippers looked over, mouthed to ask if she was OK. She nodded, then followed Jack out of the church.

She scanned the alley; there was no sign of him. He was gone, disappeared somewhere into the city. She looked at the object. It was ivory, carved. Medieval. Jesus on the cross, flanked on either side by two figures; saints, she presumed. The sun, moon and hand of God were carved on the upper half, and the whole thing was shiny. Well worn; years of pious fingers rubbing it. For good luck or redemption, she didn't know.

Mystified, Francesca buried the cross into her coat pocket.

CHAPTER THREE

Several more espressos and a round of sandwiches later, and Sasha had her first completed *Initial Consultation* form. She guided Joshua, Dana and Lizzie out of the museum and watched as they crossed the stone bridge that linked the old building to the city. Their shoulders were buried deep in fur-lined coats, streams of breath floating out behind them. She hadn't mentioned the gatehouse at the end of the bridge was where the city's public hangings took place; where Emily Myhill had been hanged.

The sky looked like snow. She shivered and wrapped her scarf round her shoulders, then reached for the packet of Marlboro Gold in her pocket. It was a filthy habit and one she tried to keep at bay, but despite the cold, she lit a celebratory cigarette and drew the hot smoke into her lungs. She resisted vaping on the basis she was more likely to give up real cigarettes; it hadn't happened yet.

The main body of the museum, a 12th-century Norman keep, loomed over her. It dwarfed the 19th-century prison buildings that stood next to it and dominated the city skyline; a giant square eye watching over the inhabitants of Norwich, day and night. A gust of cold air eddied round the old building, biting at her fingers. She ground the half-smoked cigarette into the flags beneath her feet and strode back through the entrance. A pile of damp confetti had coalesced in the relative calm of the doorway. Commercialism was the name of the game these days: weddings at the castle, the chance to be a princess for 45 minutes, was lucrative. She hoped the HRS would hold its own.

As she came in, the young woman on visitor reception beckoned to her.

'The Thomson twins are in again,' she whispered, eyes glancing towards the seating just beyond the foyer. 'They seem cross as usual. Do you want to speak to them, or should I get hold of Dr Sloucher?'

Sasha rolled her eyes. It seemed the natural law of things that something as positive as meeting Joshua, Dana and Lizzie should be offset with a visit from the Thomsons.

'It's OK,' she said. 'I'll talk to them.'

Brian and Charlie Thomson, metal detectorists, were regulars at the museum, brought objects in for identification, mostly so they could authenticate them to sell on, from what Sasha could work out. They were generally aggressive.

Drawing in a breath, Sasha approached the brothers. They stood up. Charlie, the larger of the pair, held his cap in his hand exposing a dwindling tuft of dark hair. His round face was red. Brian, the slimmer, wirier brother, had a face like a cross between a fox and a weasel, and as far as Sasha knew, a record for GBH. He stepped forward. No handshake.

'Dr Miles.' His voice was nasally, breath scented with garlic. 'I'm afraid that the museum has failed to return a number of objects owned by my brother and myself. Valuable objects.'

Sasha felt her heart sink; it was not the first time she'd heard these words from Brian.

'Are you going to find them for us?' he asked. 'Or do I need to contact the police?'

Louise Mangos lives and writes on a Swiss Alp. Her debut psychological thriller *Strangers on a Bridge* was published with HQDigital in 2018. Her second novel *The Art of Deception* was published in summer 2019. She has been a finalist in the Exeter Novel Prize and longlisted for the Bath Novel Award. Her short fiction has won prizes, been published in various anthologies, and read on BBC radio. There are links to some of these on her website:

www.louisemangos.com
louisemangos@aol.com
Twitter: @LouiseMangos
https://www.facebook.com/LouiseMangosBooks/

The Edge of Obsession

Sandrine my love,

I have been protecting you on your journey in the certainty that one day you would see the strength in our relationship. We could have been invincible together, the perfect union. Instead you have destroyed me. My world has imploded knowing you'll never be mine. I can't live without you.

Please remember me as a man who adored you from the moment he saw you until his dying breath. I'm doing this one last thing for you.

They say drowning is the most comfortable way to die, that I'll feel no pain.

I love you so much.

Yours forever,
Jake

I've arranged to have coffee with my best friend in the Café Tivoli on the main street in Châtel St Denis, but the waitress approaches me with a frown as I enter. Valérie has phoned to leave a message to say she can't make it.

'A problem with her car she needs to fix,' the waitress says. 'She told me to look for a woman with a baby.'

I curse Valérie under my breath. She has no idea how much co-ordination it takes to get out of the house, and I've been looking forward to a good chat. My spare time is precious, between the turmoil of feeding and laundry, not helped by a disturbed sleep pattern and my father who has dementia.

Kai's fallen asleep, and the smell of roasting coffee beans is alluring, so I decide to stay. At this stage the baby still sleeps for most of the day. Although I should be taking advantage and resting too, it feels good to be out. My brother's girlfriend, Marianne, is looking after Papa today, and I feel a guilty relief at being away from the house. Papa's frailty and ever decreasing moments of lucidity have recently heightened my post-natal anxiety.

The café is crowded, and my spirits fall as I scan the room, then lift again on spotting a free table in the corner by the window. Manoeuvring between seated customers, the pram labels me as a new mother, as the blue canvas hood is pristine from its recent purchase from *Mon Bébé* with my dwindling savings. We haven't been out much and I feel inept, like a learner driver on her first lesson. I bump into the back of chairs, causing sighs of protest and irritated glances.

Someone brushes past me. He waves his hand to placate customers who are obliged to move out of the way and makes my passage to the table smooth. Flushed with gratitude, I turn to thank my saviour.

'*Merci, Monsieur.*'

He tips his head, then points to the seat opposite mine.

'May I?' he asks.

I smile when I hear his accent. American, or maybe Canadian. It's hard to tell, even after all those months globetrotting with hordes of North American backpackers.

I can't stop the rush of attraction. His blond hair flops over his blue eyes, and I can tell he's well-built under his linen shirt. As a single mother, my sole purpose should be to nurture my baby for these first uncertain weeks, so I'm a little abashed for reacting to this man's attention.

Before he slides into the seat, he picks up Kai's muslin that's fallen to the floor and hangs it over the handle of the pram. He leans down and peers in.

'He's a beautiful baby,' he says.

Like any other North American tourist, he assumes we all speak English. I smile.

'Thank you, on behalf of the baby,' I say. 'He's called Kai.'

A shadow flits across his features.

'That's an interesting name,' he says as he tips his head.

He takes a seat and smiles back at me. His teeth are straight and white. Like a film star. I narrow my eyes and study his face, thinking I might have seen him on the cinema screen. He holds out his hand.

'I'm Scott,' he says. 'It's real nice to meet you.'

'Sandrine. But you can call me Sandy.'

His grip is strong, confident.

'Sandy ...' he murmurs.

The way he says my name makes me tingle. I pull at my creased blouse and suck in my stomach, still soft from carrying Kai.

'Kai was the name of the baby's father,' I say. 'But we lost him before the little one was born.'

It isn't exactly a lie, but it feels weird saying this out loud to a stranger.

Scott will probably excuse himself and take off at any moment. It isn't the first time in the past few weeks I've felt an overwhelming need to cry for no reason. Something to do with the burden of hormones.

But he reaches across the table and puts his hand on my arm. A Patek Philippe watch flashes at his wrist.

'Then it sounds like someone should be taking care of you,' he says.

I clear my throat and pick the neutral subject of the weather to try and cover my blush.

'It hasn't snowed much yet this season. Last year when I was away on my travels, the Alps experienced the coldest temperatures on record.'

'I only arrived a few months ago for work, so it looks like we've both picked the right year to be here,' he says.

The awkward moment passes, and we continue the small talk. By the time we've finished our coffees, Kai begins to fuss, and I reach for my purse. Scott wants to pay, but I insist on splitting the bill. Outside the café he asks if he can give me a lift home in his car, pointing to a black Range Rover in one of the parking spaces near the *Place d'Armes*.

I marvel at his chivalry, although it seems a bit forward for someone he's just met. I nevertheless refuse, thinking of Kai's safety without a car seat. After we swap phone numbers, he helps me lift the pram onto the bus, and says he'll call soon. I'm sure that's the end of my Cinderella meets Prince Charming moment.

'Must be the pheromones I'm giving off,' I joke with Valérie later on the phone.

'Do you fancy him?' she asks.

'He was rather lovely. I guess I do. Makes a change to meet someone sophisticated and solvent.'

'You deserve a little attention after your nightmare last year, Sand,' Valérie says, and I shiver. 'He sounds different from all those backpacking hippies.'

Valérie hums a few bars of Roy Orbison's *Pretty Woman* and mentions something about finding a rich handsome suitor to sweep me off my feet. I don't think any more of it; I'm sure Scott won't call. I figure he was simply enjoying a conversation with a young woman in a coffee shop.

CHAPTER TWO

But he does call, after only a few days. We arrange to meet in Vevey on a market day when he says he has time off work. It's a mild winter morning, and we walk along the shore of Lac Léman and through the old town, while Kai fusses in the pram. Scott doesn't seem bothered. The bustle of the market with accordion music filtering down the alleyways between the stalls drowns Kai's colicky crying.

'How're you doing?' Scott asks.

I marvel at his calmness with the baby screeching in the pram.

'A little tired,' I say. An understatement. 'I think Kai's still hungry. I need to find somewhere to feed him.'

I force a smile. In truth the smell of vegetable scraps, overripe fruit, and caustic textile dye is making me feel a little ill. And in my new role as a mother, I have no idea how to play out what is effectively our first date.

Scott places his hand lightly on the small of my back as we navigate our way through the crowds. When he helps guide the pram out of the way of a child on a scooter, I turn to thank him for these little kindnesses, and my stomach does a flip as our eyes meet.

Away from the market, we find an empty bench on the promenade by the lake where I breastfeed Kai under a shawl. Scott pulls the cloth across my shoulder when a gust of wind blows it away, and tactfully averts his gaze. We share a bottle of apple juice, and a cheese *ramequin* he bought from the bakery stall. He breaks off morsels of the little quiche and hands them to me.

'Tell me about growing up in the States,' I say.

He shrugs.

'Not much to tell. A typical American upbringing. High school. College. After I graduated, I got a job at a bank in Chicago. A couple of years later I was offered a contract in Geneva. I love Switzerland. It's like living in a fairy tale. All this alpine quaintness. I could see myself staying on, perhaps renewing my contract.' He pauses. 'But I don't want to talk about me. I want to find out about you.'

There are dark moments of my round-the-world journey last year I don't want to share with anyone. Grim memories that are best forgotten. I think about what I might share with him about myself.

'Where did you learn to speak English?' he continues before I speak. 'Your accent is perfect.'

'I went to a private bilingual school. Up there. You can see the building just below the forest.' I point to a turreted building on a slope above the town.

'Looks expensive.'

'An uncle of ours emigrated to Australia years ago. He made a fortune running a sheep station in Queensland. Although he had kids of his own, he set up a trust for my brother and me for our education. Probably felt guilty about leaving my father here to run the family farm.

'Did you enjoy it?'

'We had a great childhood – it was fun. Now I've seen more of the world, I really appreciate that.'

'What did you do when you graduated from school?'

'I had OK grades and had a few offers of places at university here and in the UK. But I decided to save up to travel first. I intended to re-apply after the year off, but came back with something a little unexpected ...'

I lift Kai in my arms as I say the word 'unexpected' and press my lips against his silky head.

'Where did you travel?' Scott asks.

I don't want him to ask about my backpacking trip. So, I remain vague about the journey, giving him a brief itinerary. When I mention America, New Zealand, Australia and Asia, a muscle ticks in his cheek. I wonder what he thinks of the whims of a girl who doesn't know what to do with her life and has carelessly allowed herself to get pregnant.

'Let me drive you home,' he says.

'That's a kind offer. But I don't want to put Kai in a car without a proper baby seat. You probably think I'm being over-protective ...'

'What would you say if I told you my neighbour had a car seat whose kid grew too big for it, and I asked to borrow it?'

'Are you serious?'

I warm to his thoughtfulness and wonder what Valérie would say. Probably that Scott must really fancy me if he's prepared to go this far.

I lift Kai out of the pram and carry him to the car seat in the back of Scott's Range Rover. I'm impressed with the state-of the-art Maxi Cosi. It's the current in-thing for yuppie parents with infant equipment budgets way above my own. It looks brand new, but I don't say anything. I'm amazed he's done this for me, on the off-chance he can drive me home. I click the buckles around Kai's little body. My fatigue and guilt are forgotten in this new hopeful excitement.

I settle into the passenger seat, enjoying the smell of new leather, and stroke the polished walnut inlay of the dashboard. My brother Pierre will be jealous about me getting a ride in this modern offshoot of our farming vehicles.

'Are you interested in seeing my place?' Scott asks as he starts the engine.

I press my lips together. This is going fast.

'OK,' I say after a pause. 'Just a few minutes. I have to get the little guy home.'

We drive up through the terraced vineyards above Lac Léman, with snow lying in little drifts in the rows between the gnarled dormant vines. On the outskirts of the village of Chardonne, Scott pulls up in front of a duplex apartment. It is constructed mostly of glass on the south side, taking maximum advantage of the spectacular view across the lake to the snowy French peaks.

'Holy shit!' slips out of my mouth before I can stop it.

'No cursing,' he says jokingly, turning to look at Kai asleep in the car seat.

Scott unlocks the door and with Kai still in the Maxi Cosi hanging in the crook of my elbow, we walk into a stunning modern interior. I imagine my mother tapping under my chin with her hand and remember to close my mouth. I've just walked into the house of my dreams.

'J P Morgan is a generous company to work for,' Scott says, seeing my expression. 'They take care of everything. My personal health and welfare.'

I try not to sound eager when he asks if I want to look around. The four bedrooms are tastefully decorated in the earthy colours I love. Everything looks fresh and new. *How perfect,* I want to say, and then think it might look like I'm coming on a bit strong.

'How long have you been here?'

'A couple of months. I lived in a condo in Geneva for a while until I decided to move to somewhere less urban.'

'That's a bit of a commute. You'll never use half these rooms. Unless you have family to stay. Don't you feel lost in this place?'

'Would you like a tea, coffee, something else?' he asks, brushing off the question.

As we walk to the kitchen, I wonder not for the first time what on earth a guy like this is doing flirting with someone like me. But as I place the Maxi Cosi on the slate-tiled floor, I choose not to question his motives too closely. I surely deserve a little attention?

As I stand up, Scott holds my shoulders. He gazes into my eyes, and my heart spikes with the intensity of his look. He kisses me tentatively. I don't react immediately, and he pulls away, a little embarrassed. I grab his shirt and kiss him back. He presses his body against mine, and I feel his passion against my hip. As we draw apart, I stand on my toes to whisper 'tea, please' hoarsely in his ear.

CHAPTER THREE

'Are you sure about this guy, Sandrine?' Marianne asks later when I describe our day out. 'Isn't it weird he's coming on so strong? I mean, you have such a young baby.'

Scott drove me home and dropped me off after we finished our tea. Marianne is sitting at the table in the farm kitchen cradling Kai in her arms while I cook dinner.

'I can't pass on this, not when he seems so keen. I just wish Kai was a little older. I feel so frumpy and tired right now.'

'You're a good-looking woman, Sandrine, whether you're a mother or not. What does he do for a living? You don't want him suddenly running back to the States because his contract has finished.'

'He told me his assignment with J P Morgan could be renewed. He's sure they'd offer him a local contract if he requested it. Look, I know you're trying to protect me ...'

'I don't want to see you get hurt, that's all.'

'I'll be fine. Don't worry. My focus is on Kai's wellbeing now.'

Marianne smiles and hugs Kai to her. Her movement makes his body quiver in his sleep. I wonder whether he's making her feel broody. Since my early return from travelling I feel like I'm encroaching on Pierre and Marianne's relationship. After Kai's arrival I've rarely been on hand to help with Papa's care, although in normal circumstances I might have moved out by now, either for study or work.

'You're very kind to me, Marianne. I'm so grateful you've accepted all this.'

I turn back to the stove and worry not for the first time how the hell I am going to support Kai and myself financially.

In the meantime, it's good to have the attention of a handsome man, no matter how fleeting.

Our courtship is a whirlwind – the old cliché. I get the feeling Scott wants to take the relationship further, but there's the uncomfortable matter of my recent birth to consider. 'I've been waiting for someone like you all my life,' is how he often puts it.

He sometimes holds Kai and studies him intently. I'd like to believe if he's falling for me, he'll fall for my baby too. I remain a little hesitant, but know things are getting serious. Adding up the positives, I want to give him more.

'He wants to take me to Paris!' I tell Pierre and Marianne when Scott drops me at home after a night out.

I dance around Kai who's sitting in his baby bouncer gumming his fist, waiting for his bedtime feed. He jumps at my squeal, and when I kiss him on the forehead, he scrunches up his eyes as a lock of my hair tickles his nose. His mouth widens into his first real smile, and I take it as a sign.

'And you're coming with us,' I say to him. 'I told Scott I couldn't possibly leave you behind, and he said of course you can come, little man, can you believe it?'

'He didn't suggest you leave him with us for the weekend?' Marianne asks.

'I'm still breastfeeding. I couldn't leave him behind. Oh, Marianne, it's like something out of a romantic movie. Paris! A dream come true.'

'I'm guessing he wants something you haven't given him yet, hey sis?' Pierre says with a theatrical wink.

After checking into a spacious suite at the Plaza on the Champs Elysées, we set out on foot to discover the city. Our visit to the Louvre is abandoned when Kai begins to cry, his wailing magnified in the great halls. Scott is a gentleman and doesn't complain about cutting short the tour.

We take a ride on a *Bâteau Mouche*. The vibration of the motor and the gentle rocking on the waters of the Seine send Kai into a deep slumber. Scott takes us to Saint Germain to buy clothes, shoes, jewellery and expensive infant outfits.

Returning to the hotel in the late afternoon, I organise a babysitter. Not wanting to be far away from Kai, I ask Scott if we can eat at the restaurant downstairs. I later find out the chef holds three Michelin stars, and tables are usually booked months in advance. How Scott manages to secure a reservation is beyond me. A financial incentive must have crossed the maître d's palm. It certainly isn't Scott's bumbling attempt to converse in French. But we are nevertheless welcomed like royalty.

The scene is set with a bottle of champagne, the sparkling art deco lights of the dining room, and every mouthful of food a sensual experience itself. Scott is initially sceptical about the tiny portions on his plate, but I know his desire for something else is replacing his appetite. And nervousness is blunting the edge to my own. We stand at the foot of the bed. As Scott's kisses grow bolder, I know there's no turning back. He takes off his shirt without removing his mouth from mine, and his chest pushes against me. This invokes a flicker of pleasure I'm determined to hold on to.

He lays me gently down on the bed. Raw passion flashes in his eyes as he gazes at my body dressed in the new Chanel night shift he bought me this afternoon. I'm glad to be horizontal, my tummy flattened by gravity. I want to feel sexy. I pray my breast milk doesn't choose this moment to stain the oyster silk.

He slowly removes the garment, the material caressing my body. I lift my shoulders as he pulls it over my head. Throwing the shift to the floor, he kisses my neck under my ear, and moves his lips across my throat. And there it is, the spark I have so craved, clenching my belly, ready for him.

'Oh Sandy,' he whispers. 'I have waited so long for you.'

I smile, glad we can finally give ourselves to each other. He carefully enters me.

'Is it OK? Are you OK?' he asks.

I nod, and his passion begins slowly and languorously, but soon quickens to a rhythm I know I can't match. But this isn't the moment to stop his ardour. I can't have it all the first time. More than anything I want to please him.

As his movements become more urgent, I begin to feel a little sore.

Scott senses my body's reluctance and slows his rhythm. Still inside me, he moves his lips from my mouth to the dip at the base of my throat. I think of Kai, sleeping soundly in his cot in the suite's sitting room next door, and how much I want a normal life with love and security for him. And a fleeting thought: *Don't wake up now.*

Scott gently tugs my hair to expose more of my throat. His lips feather my skin, and there it is again, the building of desire. When I close my eyes, the vision of my baby's father – Kai senior – swims into my thoughts. A little guiltily, I hold on to his image, snippets of memory of our time together helping to intensify the mounting passion. My head falls back onto the pillow, my breath shortens, and my heart quickens.

Scott's fingers rest briefly on my collar bone, then grip my shoulder, his thumb sinking into the hollow between the clavicle and the muscle. As his grasp triggers an almost sweet pain, his hot breath whispers in my ear: 'Now you are truly mine.' A shock courses through my body, a taser of memory.

Suddenly I am right back on that beach in Thailand the year before.

CHAPTER FOUR – JUNE 1986

'I feel guilty leaving you to deal with the farm,' I said.

Pierre and I were sitting in the café outside the departure lounge at Geneva Airport with time to kill before my flight.

'Don't start that again,' he said. 'Seriously, don't worry about us. I know it was never your intention to stay on the farm, and nobody else expects you to. Papa's pretty much stabilised. The help from the clinic is working out fine. And Marianne is happy the therapist's visits to the farm means we're not overloaded with technical medical shit. Just have a great time and keep in touch. I'm only a little jealous.'

The word 'jealous' made me feel guilty, despite his jovial tone. He had as much right to a year off as I did.

'Would you have done this if our roles were reversed?' I asked.

'The farm is my future now, Sandrine. And if things work out with Marianne, well ... it's a great basis for building a family. And I couldn't leave the girls.'

He meant the dairy herd.

'I used to lie in the back paddock next to the river in summer, watching vapour trails criss-cross the sky,' I told him. 'It's like I have to get this travel bug out of my system.'

'You can always pick up your uni applications again later. By the time you apply you'll have the last couple of years' work experience to add to your CV. Count this as a belated gap year.'

'I can hear Mama now, rolling in her grave telling me I could do so much more with my *Maturité Gymnasiale.*'

'She never intended you to stay on the farm either.'

'But she never intended me to earn quick money as a temp. I remember her voice. "You're wasting your life. You'll never get a decent job!"'

'At least the old man should appreciate the ambition. Perhaps he thinks he can participate vicariously.'

'I think Papa approves. When I told him I was going, he smiled and squeezed my hand. It was as though he was giving me permission.'

That had been a day when I doubted my decision. There were weeks when he didn't speak, and there were weeks when he ranted about people we hardly knew. There were weeks when he recognised us for seven days in a row, followed by weeks when we were all an evil alien imposition in his life.

But I had the feeling he wanted me to do this thing. I had been determined to work and save money to travel. My language skills ensured a constant supply of employment. Over two years I had amassed a decent fund, although my budget would be tight. I finally had a brand-new backpack, a pair of sturdy hiking boots, and a round-the-world plane ticket in my pocket.

My flight was announced. We rose from the table, and I hugged Pierre.

The excitement was mounting. It was time to head west into the sunset.

CHAPTER FIVE

We are two hundred feet above San Francisco Bay when I set eyes on you. I'm driving towards Sausalito across the Golden Gate Bridge, and there you are, halfway between the two great towers. I'm drawn to your blonde curls swirling in the wind. The tug of an ever-present memory. You stand stock still, and in that moment, I'm struck with the similarity your face has to the grainy black-and-white picture wedged into the air vent on my dash. Ma.

Your knuckles strain white against the straps of your backpack. As I pass by, I keep staring at your image diminishing in my rear-view mirror, throwing the occasional look back to the road in front of me so I don't drift over the lanes. I know you've experienced a surge of terror as you glance through the mesh gaps next to the sidewalk to the waves of the Pacific white-capping into the bay below you. I know, because I did that too, the first time I crossed the bridge on foot several weeks ago. I remember thinking Pa would have called me a sissy-boy.

Apart from the uncanny likeness to a mother I haven't seen for sixteen years, it's our first connection, that same fear. I remember the tremble and swing of the bridge, and the dizziness in my head when I believed I was about to die. I know you want to lie down to stop the swaying. But the potential embarrassment of surrounding witnesses, and the thought of that vertiginous drop makes you wish you could fly to the safety of solid land instead. I want to stop the car and offer you a ride but know I would cause mayhem in the middle of the heavy freeway traffic.

Instead I park my car at Vista Point, in the hope of catching sight of you, to mentally encourage you to continue your journey safely. But I can't see you from the foreshortened angle of the suspension cables stacked against each other in my line of vision. I'm impatient, and a little worried, so I climb in my car and drive back across the bridge.

By the time I reach you, your moment of terror has passed and you're striding along, gaze fixed ahead, your demons expunged. As I approach in the far lane, the oncoming traffic periodically blocks my vision. I see you laugh out loud, most likely at the ridiculous moment of fear. And then you toss your sun-bleached curls back in the wind, exposing your slender throat. The tug of longing for my mother is replaced by something more feral, an instant primeval spark. In that one witnessing of your raw, wild freedom, I fall for you. Hard. It's as though you are already part of me. I've seen your moment of weakness. Your vulnerability.

And I know I have to protect you forever.

I grew up in a dead-end town on the dusty plains of Kansas, the Rocky Mountains a mythical temptation to the west. In the winter the mountains seemed more attainable. I used to believe I could see them, shining on the horizon with a new coating of snow. In reality I probably only saw a band of clouds in the distance, held there by geography.

Ma died when I was about five years old. Cancer. I was too young to know what was going on, though I knew something tragic had happened. I remember crying at the funeral and for several days afterwards. A week later, Pa told me to buck up and stop my snivelling. It was time for me to be a man. At five, for Chrissakes!

I kept a photo of Ma in the drawer beside my bed. Every night I took it out, touched her face, asked her to keep me safe, and said goodnight to the most beautiful woman I ever knew, to the *only* woman I ever knew.

Pa mostly went on drinking binges for a couple of years, and I became accustomed to the back of his hand across my face. But he never met anyone new, which is a damn shame, as things might have been different for me growing up as an only child if there'd been a woman in the house.

Hitting wasn't all Pa's hands were used for.

Elizabeth Saccente has over thirty years' professional involvement with Japan. Her novel *Ikumo* was shortlisted for the Debut Dagger in 2006.

author@elizabethsaccente.com

pax japonica

TŌJI

Winter Solstice, 1989, Bōsō Peninsula

Choose, they said.

But he wasn't equipped to choose. They should know that. Everything in his life – education, marriage, career – had been dictated by family, culture, and, ultimately, tragedy. Even in love he'd been passive, refraining from pursuit despite his longing, deferring to duty.

That, she would have said, was a choice in itself. As was his inability to abandon the vendetta that ruled his life. Their lives.

The memory of their last conversation sliced through him: You think I don't understand? Giri. Duty. Honour. Whatever you want to call it? What about your duty to me? To our—

She'd choked up, fighting tears. Perhaps if she'd said, *'To our child'*, he'd have been forced to acknowledge an overriding obligation. But it was left unspoken, like so much.

And now this. She, and the babe she carried, felled by his fault if not his hand.

Only one can survive, they said.

Choose.

I – 7th December 1989, Nezu

Kachin. Kachin.

The clack of the fire patrol's warning blocks ricocheted through darkened lanes and into Gina Knight's consciousness, rousing her from contemplation of a grainy photo marked 'Hell's Pocket, 2nd July 1944'. The noise was intended to alert residents preparing for bed to any stray spark that could set the city ablaze, a particular danger here in Nezu and neighbouring Yanaka where so many old wooden structures, miraculous survivors of earthquake and war, remained.

Gina straightened up, stretching her arms and shoulders back to relieve the tension of hours spent hunched over, sifting through documents, notes and photos. She glanced at her watch.

'Gosh. Eleven already,' she said, prompting Professor Robert Peet, sitting opposite, to look up.

'I've kept you late,' said the Professor, bending his neck to the right and then the left. His eyes, in daylight a remarkable shade of turquoise, looked washed out and ringed with tiredness.

'Not at all. Kei's supposed to meet me. He's the one who's late.'

Nonetheless, guilt plucked at Gina's conscience. Professor Peet was elderly and they had only stopped for a fifteen-minute supper at six. She should have suggested they finish much sooner, but she'd become so immersed she hadn't noticed the time passing.

The Professor's desk was vast, battleship-grey steel. Something he'd rescued from US military surplus. Like himself, he would joke, brushing at his buzzcut, battleship-grey hair. He'd been teaching History at Tokyo University – more commonly known as Tōdai – for thirty-seven years, but 'once a Marine, always a Marine,' he liked to say.

Neither the Professor, who was at least six-foot-four, nor the desk fitted very well into what must once have been a storage loft in the old merchant-style house. There was just enough space for Gina, five-foot-two, to squeeze in across from him so that he could slide over the pages he wanted examined.

The building shuddered in a cold wind that all but negated the kerosene heater's effectiveness. Gina shivered and reached for her jacket, an insubstantial designer piece utterly wrong for the occasion. She could have dressed casually – the Professor was in jeans and a navy pullover – but she'd worn her favourite suit for luck on the first day of a new job. Even if it was just a temporary one.

The Professor stood and went to the window. 'Wow. The snow's piling up out there. Rare for Tokyo. If Kei's coming from police headquarters it might well delay him.'

Gina nodded and began tidying the papers on the desktop, stacking them neatly, squaring the corners the way a military man would like. It was quite satisfying. 'I'm really going to enjoy this project. So riveting. I mean, we studied the war in grad school, of course, but to read your first-hand account ...'

The only light in the room came from two goose-necked lamps trained on the documents, so the Professor's head was in shadow. But his American Midwest-accented voice was warm. 'I'm lucky you were free. I don't have the patience for all the fact-checking and detail work anymore.'

Just as Gina opened her mouth to respond, they heard a door slide open down below.

'That must be Kei,' said Gina, reaching for her handbag.

But the voice that called in at the *genkan* wasn't Kei's. Could not be Kei's. There came no polite '*Konban wa*' in his sonorous bass, but rather a raspy, demanding, '*Oi*, come here'. They could hear Mrs Peet's slippers shuffling along the hall and her querulous voice asking, 'Who's there?'

Gina looked at the Professor with raised eyebrows.

'I'll just go see,' he said, frowning.

The study was above the entrance to the house, but the steep, narrow stairs to reach it came from the back. He couldn't have been even halfway down them when his wife began to shout.

'What are you doing? No. Stop that. Get out. Get out of here.'

Gina's heart clutched.

The intruder's shrill invective burst through the floorboards. She caught random words – '*sonnō jōi*' '*ichioku gyokusai*' – that made no sense to her. But the tone was clearly hateful.

She grabbed the phone, an old rotary, and dialled 1-1-0, holding her breath as the dial click-click-clicked its way back from the zero.

A loud thump. A woman's cry.

'Sanae? I'm coming,' yelled the Professor. 'Sanae, what—'

The operator was asking which emergency service she wanted.

'Police. Someone's breaking in. Nezu, *ni-chome* ... I ... I don't know the number. Professor Peet. Professor Robert Peet's house.'

Gina sniffed. What was that?

The Professor's voice, frantic. 'NO. STOP.'

The smell grew stronger. It was kind of sweet, evocative ...

'Gasoline,' she shouted into the mouthpiece and dropped the phone.

II – Yanaka

Kenzo Peet balanced on the wooden track of sliding doors that had been left ajar. He'd been in the house before, quick raids into the kitchen, mainly, but this was the first time he dared go so far inside. The doors were made of smooth, dark wood slatted so that light from the hall behind him fell on the *tatami* in long, thin rectangles. The room was bare. Nothing like he'd imagined: where were the floor cushions? the low tables? the paper lanterns? There wasn't even an ancestral sword on a stand in the alcove like he'd seen on TV at the hostel. Disappointing.

If he hadn't been watching for days, if he hadn't seen the detective leave through the front gate earlier, if he hadn't heard the Old Man coughing in his bedroom at the opposite end of the house, he would think the place abandoned. It wasn't even any warmer inside than out. Go on or go back? *Never go back*, his gang would shout. They'd explored (and tagged) plenty of derelict barns and farmhouses back home. Even a condemned tractor factory one time.

The next set of doors were closed, covered in some white-ish material; he had no clue what was beyond. A closet, maybe? Another empty room? He'd have to slide one of the doors open, but not far. He was the skinny kid who slithered through gaps in fences and opened gates for the others. Their *ninja*. The best one in Iowa. The *only* one in Iowa. Better than being some goofy, buck-toothed Long Duk Dong with no friends at all.

He shook off the pang of homesickness and stepped down into the room. The floor mat creaked. A familiar scent, like just-baled hay, rose up, jolting him home yet again: Uncle Joe calling for help in the barn; their last quarrel. 'You're not my father,' he'd shouted at the kind and gentle man who'd raised him.

The argument was the whole reason he'd been living off his wits in Tokyo for the last ten days. Once he turned eighteen in the summer, he figured he had a right to know the truth about his father and his Japanese family. Aunt Em and Uncle Joe might have been his legal guardians, but they wouldn't tell him anything without Naomi's say-so. They even claimed not to know, but Kenzo didn't believe that. Besides, Naomi – she never let him call her

'Mom' – was never around, always off jet setting somewhere. 'Work,' she called it. And anyway, whenever he'd tried asking, her head would just about explode. 'He wants nothing to do with you. Nothing. You don't need to know.'

She'd never tell him. So, when the Explorers started planning a winter survival campout, he made his own plans to sneak off to Japan. He had another week before his aunt and uncle would miss him and then his buddy, Jack, would give them the letter he'd written. *Sorry, Uncle. I'll be back. Maybe.*

Of course, it was the straw of the *tatami* he was smelling, reminding him of home. A real Japanese, even a burglar, would probably have taken his sneaks off, but Kenzo needed to be ready for a quick exit. He could easily outrun the Old Man if he had to. Even so, he stood still, holding his breath, listening. There was that same faint coughing, nowhere near. He glanced at his digital watch – a supercool Casio F-91W Uncle Joe had given him for his birthday. 23:01. He moved again, three long-legged strides to reach the doors – rough paper with random gold flecks – and pushed one aside, less than a foot, making only the softest rattling. Angling his body sideways, he slipped through.

This space was dark with just a glimmer coming through the gap he'd made. He went further in, letting his eyes adjust until he could see the outline of two cushions on the floor in front of a big dresser set into a recess in the wall. The top half of the dresser – what Aunt Em would call a 'tallboy' – had doors that were wide open to reveal two shelves. On the upper one was one of those funny fat Buddha statues in what looked like gold. Next to it was a smaller stone figurine, a baby-faced god wearing a red bib and holding a miniature pinwheel. He'd seen plenty of bigger versions in the cemetery. Something to do with dead kids, he'd overheard a tourist say.

On the lower shelf were several framed photos. An old woman in black and white. A younger woman in colour, but with old-fashioned hair. And a middle-aged man, similar to but not the one he was observing. The fourth picture was small, one of those old Kodak snapshots like Aunt Em had in her albums. A couple with a toddler in a rowboat. He drew closer, squinted, reached for it.

The pale beam of light vanished.

'*Anoo ...*'

Kenzo turned.

The Old Man stood in the doorway.

Why was Tokyo never ready for snow?

Detective Superintendent Kei Shimizu knew the answer. Most winters the ridge of mountains that ran down the centre of Honshū snagged the moisture-laden air from Siberia and got buried metres deep, sparing the metropolis. But sometimes the winds came from the south, skirting the massifs. Then it was Tokyo's turn. Even the lightest snowfall wreaked havoc, and this one was intensifying fast. Thick flakes fell steadily, settling on the few frozen centimetres already covering the pavements, the towering stone walls of the imperial moat opposite police headquarters, and the stationary, bumper-to-bumper traffic on the eight-lane road in between.

'Boss, wait.'

Kei turned at the sound of Sergeant Tanaka's voice. She was charging across the lobby, hair flying as she tried to pull on a woollen bobble hat.

'I'm off duty, Tanaka,' Kei said, 'and in a hurry.'

'Boss, I can drive you,' Tanaka said when she reached him.

He chuckled, relieved. 'You love all this, don't you?' He waved a hand at the scene outside.

The Snow Country-raised sergeant grinned, causing the still raw, line-of-duty scar that bisected her left cheek to bunch up.

'I know you can drive in it, Tanaka. But no one else can. There will be accidents, abandoned cars, blocked roads. I'm late as it is. I was supposed to pick up Gina at eleven and it's –' he looked up at the big wall clock and sighed, '– eleven. I'll take the underground and I suggest you do, too.'

'But, Boss,' Tanaka said, 'you hate the underground.'

He grimaced acknowledgement of that fact, pulled the door open and waved Tanaka through it. A gust of wind blew snow and cold into the lobby, bringing a cry of protest from the receptionists. Kei shrugged deeper into his overcoat and followed Tanaka to the Metro.

Fifteen minutes later, Kei left Tanaka holding up her badge and threatening to arrest whoever had squeezed her buttock in the packed carriage. The other passengers either had their eyes closed or were looking anywhere but at the annoyed sergeant. She nodded at Kei as they pulled into Nezu station. She didn't need his help.

Desperate to escape the smell of damp wool and mothballs that permeated the overheated train, Kei took the stairs of Nezu station two at a time, gulping fresh air as he emerged. Under the thickening white mantle, the world was silent and glowing. No traffic here. Just a few cars left at odd angles to the kerb.

But something was wrong. He stood still, letting the snow accumulate on his head and shoulders, and sniffed. The sweet, smoky scent of charcoal-roasted chestnuts and yams from a recently departed street vendor lingered thick in the atmosphere, but there were hints of more troubling odours: burning wood; roasting pork; petrol. It was not a combination that made any sense in this district so late at night and the more he inhaled, the more pronounced those smells became.

He turned a slow circle, scanning, listening.

There.

His gut clenched as he raised his eyes to curls of smoke, furling and unfurling above the rooftops, multiplying pale grey against the indigo sky. 'There' was where he was heading.

A wail of approaching sirens kindled Kei's fear. It won't be the Peets' house. It won't. But in this tinderbox town if one building went up, they were all at risk.

He set off, big strides, wanting to run but hindered by the slickness of the pavement. Fire engines and police vehicles overtook him – one, two, four – and slewed to a halt at the entrance to the lane, leaving space for the ambulance that followed to get closer to the scene.

Dozens of firemen leapt from the pumpers before they even braked, grabbing hoses, axes, an urgent but controlled choreography accompanied by a swelling masculine chorus of orders, warnings and encouragements. So many, in their brown jackets, day-glo orange stripes, operating in concert to a rhythm only too familiar to Kei.

The police set up a cordon to keep already gathering gawpers at a distance. Kei flashed his ID at the nearest patrolman and charged into the lane only to be blocked by a swarm of fleeing residents, pyjamas under overcoats, bare feet in garden sandals. Some of the firefighters had begun hosing down neighbouring houses to keep the flames from spreading. The gutter ran with ash and slush, but Kei stepped into it, oblivious to the wet and the cold, bypassing the escapees.

Peet-sensei no uchi, he heard them calling to one another as they passed clutching sleepy-eyed children. Horror for the Peets, relief for themselves. As long as the fire didn't spread.

A crash and a roar rocked the street. Glass shattered. Terracotta roof tiles hurtled to the ground. Flames shot up, blazing white hot towards the sky. Women screamed. Children cried. Kei ran.

In sight of the house he pulled up, breathing hard, aghast. It was wreathed in smoke, one side of the structure torn away, yellow tongues of fire licking at ragged splinters.

'GINA. ROBERT,' he shouted.

'*Oji*-san. *Oi*. Stop.' A thick-gloved hand landed on Kei's shoulder. '*Oji-san*, you must stand back.'

He shook the masked and helmeted firefighter's hand off, waved his own at the house. 'My family ... girlfriend ... elderly ...' He advanced.

The fireman darted forward, blocking Kei's path. Kei, a head taller and broader, shoved him aside, cutting off his: '*Dame, Oji-san*. Too dangerous—'

Kei gripped the handle of the glazed aluminium entry door – the glass had shattered, but the metal was intact – and yanked it aside, his hands so cold he didn't feel his palm sizzle. Hot, stinging smoke billowed, carrying with it the powerful smells of roasting meat and petrol he'd detected earlier. Bile rose in his throat. He knew what that meant.

Someone he loved was burning.

IV – Yanaka ▶ *Nezu*

Kenzo congratulated himself on a clean escape until he realised that the jacket he'd thrown over the glass shards at the top of the Shimizus' garden wall had torn, leaving a scrap behind. He'd scratched his arm, too, so there'd be blood. Too late to get it back now. He'd heard the Old Man shuffling about out there, muttering at first, then yapping something that sounded like 'Gotcha.'

That didn't worry him, though. The Old Man had to know he – or someone – had been in the house before, stealing food, yet there was no sign he'd ever called the cops. He even left lunch boxes inside the cemetery gate sometimes. After trying one, Kenzo left them to others who appreciated the unfamiliar fare more.

Clearing snow off a grave, Kenzo sat down to catch his breath. Yanaka Cemetery bordered the Shimizus' house and provided him with plenty of hiding places, but this was his favourite: a grouping of five stone markers surrounded by a high hedge. There was room for him to stretch out his long legs and a hollow to hide his supplies. The cemetery was so big it had its own police station – pretty weird – and patrols chased away any vagrants they encountered, but Kenzo had so far managed to evade them.

The cops would have just finished a round and wouldn't be making another for hours. Could he get away with making a fire? He had a stash of twigs that should be dry enough. But he would risk discovery. Was he ready for that?

He shivered. Uncle Joe's guidebook said Tokyo was sunny in winter, so he hadn't brought anything in the way of woolly sweaters – Aunt Em knitted him a new one every year – or waterproofs. Or sturdy footwear. The snow was coming down hard and the sleeves of the parka he'd pinched from a peg in a noodle shop barely reached below his elbows. It was too late to get into the Oke Hostel for the night. Reception closed at six and they locked the front door at ten.

Kenzo rubbed his hands together and looked around. There was a spot at the back where the hedge had overgrown. Squeezed in there, wrapped in a scavenged quilt, he'd probably be warm and dry enough for the night. He could go for a hot bath at the *sentō* first thing in the morning, then check in to the hostel.

That seemed like a plan. But he wasn't tired and he was hungry. He hadn't taken any food from the Shimizu kitchen this time, just that photo now tucked inside his jeans pocket. The noodle bar would be closed, but there were vending machines on the main road and he had cash. If he was lucky there'd be a hot drinks machine.

The crunch of the snow beneath his feet was loud in the otherwise silent lane. Every window remained dark, though. A perfect opportunity.

From his pocket Kenzo pulled a small can of red spray paint he'd discovered at the bottom of his rucksack. Kids didn't seem to do much tagging here in Japan. Not that he'd seen anyway. Maybe he'd start a trend. Maybe he'd get arrested. He didn't really think so, but if he did, he would tell them who his father was; then Detective Kei Shimizu would have to have something to do with him. Either way, it was a chance to make his mark.

He gave the can a good shake and stepped up to the stone wall. First was the 'Z' – sharp angles connected by long diagonal line, then the 'oo' – cartoon eyes looking right or left. This time he wanted to make them look right, towards the gate. But the blasted paint ran out before he could get in the last eyeball, leaving his 'Zoo' looking stupid.

'Fuck,' he muttered, tossing the can over the wall.

And now his damned sneakers were soaked and useless. His feet were blocks of ice. Why the hell did no one around here put salt on the pavements? At home that would earn a fine. Or a lawsuit if someone slipped.

His stomach rumbled. The need for food set his legs back in motion. Visibility was poor on the main road, but he could see multi-coloured lights chasing across a row of vending machines less than fifty yards away. Kenzo laughed. Why make them look like arcade games when it was cool enough that you could buy just about anything from them: candy; snacks; drinks; cigarettes, natch; but hot pot noodles? Full-sized bottles of whisky? Porn mags? Crazy.

When he reached the four vendors, he couldn't believe his luck. Heated-in-the-can soup. Rice bowls with bits of chicken or other stuff on top. French fries. Hot fucking French fries. There was even ice cream. His choice was a no-brainer. He scrabbled in a pocket for two hundred-yen coins and a fifty, dropped them in the slot and pressed the button. This set off a cacophony of bings, bongs and cartoon music that made him jump and look around, nervous that he'd waken the whole neighbourhood.

Two minutes of that and a cardboard bucket of steaming, golden fries dropped into the delivery slot. The machine noise stopped, but other sounds, louder sounds, took over. Sirens, wailing, nee-nawing, whoop-whooping, the whole cavalcade of emergency vehicles zipping past him, red and blue lights colouring the falling snow.

Kenzo watched them turn off the main road. He spotted the smoke over the rooftops. He picked up his fries and followed. Fires were exciting.

Kenzo knew this lane. He'd been down it a few times looking for his grandparents' home, but he'd yet to figure out which house was theirs. The numbering system made no sense: two next to thirty-two next to seventeen. And they weren't in a row, either, but in a block. Stupid.

There was a crowd behind police lines. Many people were wrapped in those shiny space blankets he'd seen marathon runners use to keep warm after a race. Most were staring straight ahead, mesmerised by the blaze. Kenzo knew at a glance that his grandparents weren't among them. Grandpa Peet was real tall and grey-haired. He'd stick out.

Kenzo had seen bigger fires. Old man McCarthy's barns had gone up one after the other during a summer of drought. The smell of burning hay, weatherboard, and manure hung over the neighbouring Peet farm for weeks. But this fire, what he could see of it above the mass of emergency vehicles, was white hot.

Someone nudged his arm. A smiling, snaggle-toothed old woman carrying a huge thermal jug like Aunt Em used for coffee at her bridge parties offered him what looked like steaming hot tea. He accepted it, something to warm his fingers, and thanked her.

'*Zannen desu nee?*' She said, looking at the burning house. And still smiling.

Not knowing how to answer, Kenzo nodded. He pointed to the house. 'Peet?'

The woman turned her face up to his, the smile gone. '*Hai, hai,* Peet-*sensei no uchi.*'

Kenzo knew all those words but his brain refused to compute the meaning. '*Hai*' was 'yes'. '*Sensei*' meant teacher. And '*uchi*' was home. His grandparents' home was burning, and they weren't out here. Maybe in one of the ambulances. They had to be safe somewhere.

There was a loud pop. The onlookers wailed in alarm, ducking and covering their heads as a flaming chunk of something arced across the sky, showering them with sparks.

Kenzo looked for a way past the cordon.

V – Nezu

'*Gina. Robert. Sanae.*'

Kei shouted again and again into the *genkan*. He strained his ears, both fearing and praying for an answering cry.

Somehow, in all the din, the rustle and roar of the blaze, the bellows of the fire brigade, the collapses of timbers, he detected a wail. Or a whistle. Faint, but there. He moved blindly into the foyer, closing his eyes against the acrid smoke, wrapping his hands in his coat sleeves to feel his way. The slate floor was ringed in fire, the wooden step beyond alight. A 'V' of flame was spreading into the house and the *shoji* doors were reduced to cinders.

Kei tried to cry out again, but his throat, already raw from breathing hot smoke, produced only a squawk. 'Gina? Robert? Where are you?'

The wail came again. Closer. A human sound, not just the sizzle of moisture in burning wood. He made himself still, listening. It stopped.

Sweating inside his overcoat, he inched forward, one arm over his mouth, the other shielding his eyes. He trod on something soft. Crouching, squinting, he touched what felt like thick wool. A rug? Unburnt? A fire blanket, maybe? The whistling sound came again. From beneath the blanket, he realised. And something moved.

Kei tore the covering aside to find a heap of smouldering rags. A trembling, wailing, reeking heap. Gagging, he pulled at the tatters. Inside them, a charred figure. More a horror movie special effect than a human being, its burnt limbs writhing in grotesque slow motion, a high-pitched keen emanating from a hole in the scorched face, like air slowly escaping a punctured tyre. Kei dammed his revulsion, scouring the creature for any recognisable feature. He couldn't tell if it was man or woman, young or old, nor even if it was tall or short so contracted were the extremities.

God, don't let it be Gina.

He looked for hands, jewellery. Gina wore no rings, dammit. Why hadn't he given her one?

A blast rocked the building. Dense clouds of smoke and steam billowed around him. Debris rained down. Kei shielded the burnt body with his own.

'HELP. HERE. QUICK,' he shouted.

His voice seemed lost in the shower of splintered wood and hot embers, but hands appeared. Two, then two more. Reaching for him, pulling him up, away. They yanked off his smouldering coat, wrapped him in foil, pushed a mask up to his face.

He resisted, gasping, trying to explain.

'We'll take care of him, *Oji-san*. You must go back. It's dangerous.'

He rasped out that he was a cop, his rank. No one's uncle.

'Fine. Superintendent. But it's still dangerous and you're not equipped.'

'Inside. More. Inside.'

'How many? Where?'

Coughing hard, Kei held up two fingers. 'Don't know where. Not a big house.'

The fireman nodded, turned away and called orders. A wave of acknowledging shouts saw two of the men rush off.

Kei grasped the firefighter's arm. 'I need to ... I need to know. Who that is. My girlfriend was in that house.'

'Please, Superintendent. Move back. Let us do our work.'

Kei retreated a few steps outside, planting himself where he could see what was happening. He watched the paramedics kneel by the burn victim, tear open their packs, pull out equipment. One, his hands wrapped in thick gauze pads, gingerly steadied the skull while another fed a tube into the mouth. Around them firemen scrambled to keep the blaze at bay, gradually advancing into the house.

'Superintendent?'

'Yes?'

'Captain Kanno, 6th Fire District.' The man came alongside Kei, pulled off his helmet and gave his head a shake. He had a gourd-shaped face with downturned eyes that lent him a doleful air. Kei tensed, expecting bad news. The worst news. 'I understand you know the occupants?'

'I've told them already. Professor Robert Peet. His wife, Sanae. Gina Knight. She was visiting. Working with the Professor. I was late—' Kei's mouth dried up.

Kanno blinked. 'The emergency call was made by a woman with a foreign accent. She mentioned an intruder. So we need to account for four people, including the owners, *ne*? Did you recognise the victim in the *genkan*?'

Kei shook his head. 'Impossible.'

'OK. Look, you need to get that hand treated—'

'I need to know,' Kei repeated.

More vehicles arrived, wedging themselves into the lane, spilling more firemen and paramedics. There seemed to be dozens, vanishing and reappearing as smoke and steam whirled around them. Most had tanks on their backs, masks and goggles on their faces. They pulled thick, heavy hoses or carried axes and other tools whose purpose eluded Kei. They moved in waves from one hotspot to the next, spraying and chopping. Some continued to hose neighbouring buildings to stop the fire spreading.

He watched as if in a dream, waiting for the bodies to be carried out, for this new grief to begin.

Finally, the paramedics prepared to lift the charred mass of human being. They had all wrapped their hands in gauze and positioned themselves around the victim, five in total. As they heaved, another bizarre whistle emanated from the scorched lips. For a moment everyone stopped and watched.

Bizarrely, a cheer went up from somewhere behind the house. There were calls for another stretcher. Kei's gut turned liquid. He looked towards the sounds but saw only smoke. They must have found someone alive. He ran in that direction just as a firefighter emerged cradling a small, dark-haired woman. Sanae or Gina? Which one? Which one?

Two ambulance men with a stretcher pushed Kei out of the way. As the fireman laid the woman on it, her head turned.

Gina.

She saw him, made a weak smile beneath the mask, moved her lips.

His legs wobbled.

'Gina. Thank God.' He stumbled closer.

She pulled up the oxygen mask and, with visible effort, croaked: 'You're late.'

Matthew Smith is a debut novelist. He read English at Cambridge and completed his PhD on Henry James. He has held senior digital roles in government agencies, knowledge businesses and charities. Nowadays he runs his own consultancy and lives with his family in Surrey. *In Wolf's Clothing* was longlisted for the CWA Debut Dagger 2019.

matthew@matthewsmithassociates.com

In Wolf's Clothing

It didn't take long to get on the wrong side of Sergeant Talisker.

This is the first time I've visited Scotland since Independence, but it was still disorientating to go through border control when I landed and have my luggage searched. I told the official I'm travelling to the Islands on business, but he wasn't happy when he found my handgun and started asking questions about all those interesting stamps in my passport.

Eventually I was allowed to go on my way, but not before I missed my connecting flight to Lewis. Night was already falling when the little turboprop swooped down over the Minch, so low that the fishing boats twinkled like stars in the black water below, and I set foot on Lewis for the first time in more than twenty years.

My hotel in Stornoway is a modest affair. Talisker has left a one-line message for me at reception, saying we can meet in the bar when he gets off shift. The local police know nothing about the real purpose of my visit, of course. I just have time to unpack and get downstairs before the kitchen stops serving.

Afterwards I go up to the bar for a refill and I spot a twenty-something girl waiting on her own, long red hair scraped carelessly up into a ponytail. She's checking her phone for messages, her brow contracted in an irritated frown.

The only woman in a room full of single men, but for some reason no one has made a move.

'Can I buy you a drink? I'm waiting for someone too.'

She looks me up and down appraisingly, taking in my dark Jermyn Street suit and my handmade leather shoes.

'You must be Mr Nairn. *Ciamar a tha sibh?* I'm Sergeant Talisker.'

This wasn't in the file.

'Please, just Nairn.'

Her frown deepens.

'I'll have that drink if you're still offering.'

We sit together at my table by the fire. Talisker is slim and tall, almost as tall as me. Her knees nudge the underside of the table and my drink slops onto the menu.

'Good flight?'

'Not particularly.'

'You won't enjoy tomorrow then. The forecast is rough seas and strong winds. I hope you're not planning to come dressed like that.'

'Look, let me ...'

'You must have a lot of pull, Mr Nairn.' Talisker is already bored with small talk. 'Skalfa is a place of Special Environmental Interest. It's off limits to the public and home to all kinds of – unusual wildlife. The last time *Poileas* was on the island was two years ago and that was to pick up the body of a damn fool cultist who drowned himself in the breakers. But yesterday my boss gets a call from the Norwegian Embassy, saying their man is on the next plane to Stornoway and needs immediate access to the dig site.'

'It's just a routine inspection.'

Talisker looks at me over her glass, her eyes as green and unwelcoming as the Atlantic surf. I carry on talking.

'As you know, national ownership of a number of islands was still in dispute when the independence settlement came into force. The dig on Skalfa pre-dates the Edinburgh Agreement, and the continuing presence of the archaeological team was written into the accord. Regular inspections of the site are a legal requirement.'

'What needs inspecting about a hole in the ground?'

'It's not every day archaeologists live side by side with a pack of grey wolves.'

'I haven't heard the wolves complaining.'

'We have to observe the formalities, Ms Talisker. This is a pan-European project, on Scottish soil, on an island privately owned by a foreign national. With two British subjects on site. It's a regulatory minefield.'

This explanation isn't quite as absurd as it sounds. Tensions ran high during the independence talks and the Scots mischievously laid claim to everywhere north of the original line of Hadrian's Wall. For the last few years, the inhabitants of Carlisle and Newcastle have been convinced they would end up wearing kilts.

Talisker remains unconvinced.

'And what are you, Mr Nairn? Not Norwegian, for one thing.'

I let a touch of irritation creep into my voice.

'I'm a consultant to the project: that's really all you need to know. You've seen the paperwork, officer, I have all the permissions required. I'm just impatient to get out to the island now to meet my colleagues.'

Talisker pulls a face and picks up the stained menu. She turns it over, takes a pen out of her bag and starts drawing on the back.

'I've already got a map.'

'I've lived on the Islands all my life, Mr Nairn. I was born on Lewis, my father drives the school bus and it was my brother's taxi brought you from the airport. I don't need a map of Skalfa: this is for your benefit. You can keep it if you like.'

She flips the menu around. Seen from above, the island is shaped like a swimming animal. To the north, a blunt snout, joined by a bulbous body to a thin, snaking peninsula of a tail in the south. She points to the snout with her pen.

'This is *Geal Crun*, the site of the dig. The cliffs here are steep and inaccessible, even when the sea is calm. The terrain is rough with no obvious landing spots. The mountains to the south mean radio communication is intermittent at best. The five-man team is due to complete the first stage of the excavation by Christmas. They check in a couple of times a week by sat phone with your support team in Oslo. Otherwise they rely for everything – food, supplies, fuel – on the research station here.'

She marks a cross on the end of the island's tail.

'There is a natural harbour to the south and a jetty for the occasional ferry boat from Lewis. The scientists are a semi-permanent feature, monitoring the rewilding project on the island. They have an inflatable and once a fortnight they shoot down the coast, land in one of these inlets and make a delivery. It gets pretty lonely out there, so the arrangement suits everyone.'

For someone who only found out about my arrival yesterday, Talisker is very well prepared.

'I've chartered a boat to drop us at the south end of the island. The rewilders will escort us the rest of the way to *Geal Crun*.'

I start to object but Talisker is having none of it. Skalfa is a dangerous place, she says, and she's not about to let me wander around it unsupervised. We arrange to meet on the harbour wall the next morning.

'It's dark early this time of year, so please don't be late. I aim to be on and off that island in forty-eight hours so I can get on with my real job.'

Suddenly I'm reluctant to let her go so easily.

'Won't you at least stay for a nightcap? I'll get the rest of the bottle and you can teach me some Gaelic.'

But Talisker is already on her feet.

'*Feasgar math,* Mr Nairn! I suggest you have an early night. Three hours at sea is a long time in a small boat.'

Talisker's prediction of a three-hour trip turns out to be over-optimistic.

The wind gets up and the boat heaves and yaws in the choppy waters. We wait half an hour for another police to turn up, but he calls in sick and at last Talisker loses patience and tells the captain to cast off. We soon lose sight of Lewis in the mist and St Kilda is already a vanishing dot on the horizon. Skalfa is the westernmost point of what was formerly known as the United Kingdom. It is sixty miles from the coast of Lewis and closer to Norway than London. If Talisker's numbers are right, it's home to no more than ten people.

Maybe fewer by now.

Once or twice the captain tries to turn back but Talisker is adamant. We are swept up by another wave and the entire boat rocks and shudders like a fairground ride.

Hours pass. We churn around in the slate-grey sea, hardly making any forward progress. Gannets and guillemots flit in and out of the waves like spray. My waterproofs are no match for Talisker's and already I'm wet through to my skin.

But eventually the wind starts to die down and a shaft of watery sunlight breaks through the clouds. I manage to light a cigarette successfully and stand in the bow, puffing contentedly. It's a bad habit, especially for climbers, but one I've never entirely been able to break.

Talisker joins me. Her face, what I can see of it, is pale but determined. We stand side by side as the mist begins to part and we catch our first glimpse of Skalfa, suddenly surprisingly close as if it's risen out of the ocean like a sea monster. Even from this distance, the ragged cliffs to the north of the island look impossibly steep and forbidding. The waves break on them in small explosions, making the birds scream and scatter to their hiding places on the rock face. The sea is somewhat calmer here but the horizon reels and trembles with every movement of the boat.

My head throbs the way it does when I'm climbing at altitude. We slow and turn as the captain points us southwards and I can feel the engine vibrating through the soles of my feet. Standing here, it's hard for me to believe people ever lived on Skalfa.

In fact, there was a small community on the island up until the outbreak of World War Two. The thirty or so residents of nearby St Kilda petitioned to be relocated to the mainland: the villagers of Skalfa had to be forcibly evicted by the army in the end. The island's remoteness made it an ideal spot for testing new technologies for the war effort. Even now, parts of the shoreline are still fenced off with barbed wire.

Talisker's hand-drawn map doesn't turn out to be very accurate after all. The island's 'tail' sweeps round to create a spectacular natural harbour in the shape of a horseshoe. After another hour or so of manoeuvring, we drop anchor and the captain transfers us to the jetty in a dinghy.

Relieved to be on dry land again, we disembark, dump our bags and turn to see him heading back to the boat at top speed. It'll be getting dark soon and our chaperone wants to take advantage of the turning tide.

Talisker calls after him.

'Angus! If you're not back here in two days wi' a change of clothes and calm sea, I'll have your bloody licence.'

I look around. There is no one to be seen. The jetty leads to a shallow beach of pure white sand. The sweeping granite wall of the harbour is topped with gorse and heather, giving way to steep mossy slopes spotted with rocky outcrops and the occasional stunted furze bush. There are no trees here, and no sign of a habitable dwelling.

In the distance, the white face of *Sgùrr nan Geal* is lost in cloud.

'Don't look so worried, Nairn. The wolves haven't got us yet.'

Now I see them.

Perched dangerously near the edge of the cliff are a group of small white prefabricated pods. It looks like a model for human habitation on the surface of Mars. A door opens like an eye blinking and three sets of arms are waving at us.

We have a welcoming committee.

CHAPTER TWO – SIR CHRISTOPHER

Twenty-four hours earlier, I was in London, looking forward to nothing more strenuous than Sunday lunch.

The Third Gulf War put a bullseye on the British capital. They say the clean-up at the Stock Exchange will take months, and the last drinking water scare closed every bar and restaurant in the West End. After text messages triggered another wave of terrorist bombings, government panicked and shut down the network altogether. Now it's easier to get a mobile signal on K2 than in the middle of Westminster.

I decided to give the Tube a miss, took a cab to Parliament Square and walked across the park. It was a wet autumnal Sunday morning and there weren't many people about, not counting armed policemen. I got a cup of coffee and dawdled up Pall Mall, taking my time. My outbound flight was booked; my bags, packed.

I might as well enjoy the sights.

The previous day I had spent closeted with Mother's lawyers. Afterwards I booked into a hotel for the night – the old townhouse holds too many memories – and my uncle invited me to dine with him at his club. It would be the first time we've met in two years, since he first raised the idea of the Siberian fiasco that put me in hospital for three months.

When I was a child, I remember Uncle Christopher (never 'Chris') treating my mother and me to Sunday lunch at the Ambassadors. It was a very grand occasion for a small boy. Nowadays the club still smells of roast beef, leather and cigar smoke but somehow the institution seems diminished. The carpets a little scuffed, the armchairs a little shabbier, the members a little thinner on top.

'Good morning, Mr Nairn. Let me see ... Sir Christopher is waiting for you in the Albany Room. Up the stairs and on your left, sir.'

No one knows quite what my uncle does at the FCO, but the years have obviously taken their toll. He looked as if he hadn't slept for a week, and when he stood up to shake my hand he stooped like a retired headmaster. If I had passed him in the street, I wouldn't have recognised him.

'Thank you for coming, Andrew.'

It was a fair-sized room, with book-lined walls, a view of St James's and a handsome mahogany desk in one corner. We sat by the window, a knee-high coffee table between us. There were three plain cardboard files on the table.

'Please accept my condolences, my boy,' he began.

'She was your sister.'

He carried on as if I hadn't spoken.

'I'm sorry I wasn't able to attend the funeral. It was simply impossible for me to get away from Whitehall. I'm sure you understand.'

'Not really. My mother was in no position to resent your non-appearance if that's any consolation.'

His blue eyes at least are still youthful. They glittered coldly at me now.

'How long since you went away, Andrew? Chasing wolves, living on your trust fund. You're hardly in a position to lecture me.'

'You're right, I'm not.'

'Please, hear me out. I did want to talk to you today, but not about your mother. About something much more important.'

He saw the look on my face.

'I understand this is a difficult time but believe me, Andrew, I wouldn't have invited you here if I thought there was any alternative. Let me get you a drink.'

After a long pause I sat down again. He went to the drinks cabinet and came back with two tumblers and a decanter. I left mine untouched. I was intrigued in spite of myself. My uncle isn't the sort of man who ordinarily does things for other people: that's what women and servants are for.

'Before you left,' he started again, 'you made yourself useful running some – errands – for the British government. Your father's name, your professional access to remote parts of the world, allowed you to pass undetected where conventional approaches had failed. Your efforts were helpful to me, very helpful. For the most part.'

'I don't do that sort of thing anymore. Not after last time.'

'Of course, I understand. But very recently a crisis has arisen. A crisis that calls for someone of your unique abilities, Andrew. When I heard that you were coming home, well, it almost seemed like fate.'

He opened the first file and took out a photograph.

'Do you recognise this young woman?'

The picture was of an earnest-looking girl in her teens. She was riding a bicycle, obviously unaware of the photographer. Just visible in the background was the familiar gatehouse of King's College, Cambridge. The soft white scarf thrown carelessly around her neck emphasised her dark skin.

'No, I don't.'

'Really? Well, you have been in the wilderness for a long time. Suffice it to say that it has become very important to determine the whereabouts of this young lady and return her safely to London.'

'I don't understand. Finding missing persons is a job for the police.'

'Normally, yes. But this isn't a normal situation. It is of vital importance that no one should know that she is missing, or that we are looking for her.' He looked at me searchingly. 'Are you a patriot, Andrew?'

'I don't stand up for the national anthem, if that's what you mean.'

My uncle shielded his face with his hand for a moment and for the first time it occurred to me that he was in the grip of some strong emotion. He took a sip from his drink and opened the second file.

'You're aware, of course, that the Royal Family had to give up Balmoral as part of the independence settlement. Bamburgh Castle was Her Majesty's preference. Parts of Northumbria are very like Scotland, I believe. Some official concern was expressed at the time. In retrospect, I'm sorry to say the monarch's wishes prevailed over considerations of security.'

He took out several photographs from this new file and fanned them out in front of me.

Bodies everywhere. Some I recognised: some their own mothers wouldn't recognise. I didn't need to see the bullet wounds to know that human beings did this. Only human beings kill like this.

My uncle pointed to a couple lying face down, their hands still joined.

'These two are the girl's grandparents. It was a special occasion, so a lot of important people were attending, unfortunately.'

He cleared his throat.

'We believe some members of Royal Protection had become radicalised. CCTV footage shows them turning their guns on the family. The few survivors are critically injured and unable to answer questions. You've probably read about an outbreak of food poisoning at the castle. All official engagements are being discreetly rescheduled and for the moment the media is distracted by events in the City.' He shook his head disbelievingly. 'But it's only a matter of time before the truth leaks out, Andrew.'

My uncle leaned across the table and lowered his voice.

'You see now how important this young lady has become. Of course, in normal circumstances it would be – out of the question,' he said delicately. 'But her father is not expected to live. As things stand, she may be the only thing between what is left of the United Kingdom and a major constitutional crisis. Civil disorder, even.'

Sir Christopher is a practised liar. In his job you have to be.

'I don't know what to say. This is – very shocking news. But I still don't understand why you're telling me. I'm leaving the country tomorrow. England's not my home any more. In any case, the story is bound to get out soon enough. Maybe the consequences won't be as bad as you predict.'

'Don't you see? I am breaching the Official Secrets Act simply by meeting you here today. The situation at home is much worse than you know. The country is isolated in the face of this latest wave of terror attacks. Old friends are deserting us. Dire economic news, food shortages, the imminent collapse of many public services. All of this will become clear in the next few months. We cannot afford a period of profound political instability on top of all the other challenges facing government. Andrew,

I am taking this enormous risk in speaking to you because I think you're the only person who can help.'

I began to get up for the second time.

'I'm flattered but it's really not my problem. I think you've got the wrong idea about how I spend my time nowadays. I'm much more interested in animals than people.'

To my surprise, he didn't try to stop me. Instead he gathered up the photographs and put them neatly back in the cardboard folder. Then he calmly pushed the third file across the table towards me.

'I thought you might feel like that. I could have you arrested, of course. With the information now in your possession, I can hardly allow you to leave the country.'

'Just try it.'

'There are two plainclothes policemen waiting downstairs. I expect they are missing their Sunday lunch by now. All I have to do is call reception and you can be detained almost indefinitely under the new powers. You don't even have any family left to come looking for you.'

Sir Christopher didn't look so frail now.

'You're right. Five years away, I must be out of touch. I'd forgotten just what a bastard you can be.'

'Don't be like that, Andrew. Aren't you even curious about where we think she is?'

He pushed the file towards me with his fingertip, as if it might be contaminating.

'She's on Skalfa. A tremendous cock-up by the Home Office or the Palace or Five but there we are. Ironic, isn't it? I spoke to my sister a few weeks before she died, and she told me the one place you really wanted to go was Skalfa and now you have the perfect excuse. Your flight's already booked, the local police are expecting you. You can even take that file with you and mug up on your cover story on the way.'

I took a breath.

For a moment I could almost hear the waves, taste the salt in the air.

'And what if I say no? I've been in tougher places than Belmarsh.'

'Well, we'd find someone else, I suppose, but these things take time and the princess may not have much time left. I imagine that would be difficult for you. Another death on your conscience, I mean. Given your history.'

He looked up and smiled thinly.

'Get that girl, Andrew, bring her home safely and you will have earned the thanks of a grateful nation. HMG will turn a blind eye to past indiscretions and, who knows, maybe even find some funding for your next adventure. You should be thanking me.'

'I don't need your fucking money, Chris. I've got plenty of my own.'

It's true, I don't.

But when I left the Ambassadors Club half an hour later, I had my uncle's dossier safely in my laptop bag. On my way out, I checked reception for police, but the lobby was empty now.

At the last moment I changed my mind.

Thankfully the restaurant was still serving. I like my beef done very rare. For good measure I ordered a bottle of the '89 Petrus and smiled warmly at the waitress.

'Charge everything to Sir Christopher's account, please. My uncle's treating me.'

CHAPTER THREE – WELCOME TO SKALFA

The Skalfa research station was originally designed for five people but two colleagues have recently returned to the mainland, so a couple of tiny study bedrooms are free. I stow my bag underneath my bunk and join Talisker with the three scientists in the space they call 'the den'.

The comparison with a deep space expedition turns out to be an apt one. The project is jointly resourced by the Universities of Edinburgh and Oslo and our new friends have been alone on the island for nearly a year. The living conditions are cramped and basic, with most of the space taken up by computer monitors, neat piles of notes and reference materials. Maps and charts are loosely tacked to the walls like posters in a student dorm.

The three-person team consists of two men and a woman. They profess themselves delighted to see us. Stefan and Alasdair help bring our stuff up from the beach while Dr Nilsson, the senior researcher, goes off to prepare supper.

I catch her looking curiously at me and I smile blankly back.

Over dinner the conversation turns to the purpose of the rewilding project. The research is underwritten by the Scottish government. Eco-tourism is potentially an important part of the country's future. If the experiment on Skalfa is seen to be a success, there's a real chance of wolves being reintroduced to the Scottish mainland, says Stefan cheerfully.

'You have to understand, Mr Nairn, rewilding is truly a philosophy, not a technology. We are here to do more than curate a few exotic species. We are transforming the ecology of the whole island.'

Talisker's not interested. She wants to know how early we can leave tomorrow and who will be coming with us.

Dr Nilsson sits next to me. Sigrid is in her late twenties, with delicate features and a long rope of yellow hair. The top two buttons of her shirt are casually undone. There isn't much room around the table and her thigh is pressed against mine.

'And what about you, Mr Nairn? What is your interest in Skalfa? You don't look much like a policeman.'

'Andrew, please. I'm here to check in with the dig team. To make sure their work isn't being disrupted—'

'—by the wolves? How interesting. But if your colleagues are distracted on Skalfa, I think you will find the wolves are not to blame. They mostly keep away from human beings. Your face seems familiar somehow, Andrew,' she continues, leaning closer. 'Could we have met before? Usually I have a good memory for faces.'

Stefan and Alasdair are both glaring at me now. Alasdair in particular has barely spoken since we sat down.

'I do a bit of climbing when I'm not working. Perhaps we met in the mountains one time.'

'Alasdair also considers himself a climber. His room is full of ropes and ice axes and such. He says he is going to scale the White Mountain before we leave but we are still waiting. Isn't that so, Ally? You should talk to Mr Nairn, maybe he can give you some tips.'

Stefan laughs harshly. Talisker looks as if she holds me personally responsible for the way the evening is going.

Sigrid wants to know about all the famous mountains I have climbed and sits so close I am staring straight down her cleavage. Sigrid likes to ski in Chamonix. Perhaps we met there, she suggests, or Kitzbühel or Zermatt.

'But for some reason I picture you somewhere cold and dark, Andrew. Not a resort, at all.'

I decide to change the subject.

'I see you have a gun case back there. I hope you don't have occasion to use it. The Cheyenne believe the wolf is an oracle who speaks to the dead. To kill one is to invite retribution from the pack and bring bad luck on the village.'

She holds my eyes for a moment.

'My work takes me to many wild places, Mr Nairn. In my experience, killing sometimes brings bad luck, but rarely retribution.'

She smiles innocently.

'Not at first, anyway.'

Talisker is the first to break the silence.

'Killing – of animals, you mean?'

'Of course, Sergeant, do not worry! But we are all animals, in the end. Pack animals, like my little research family here.'

Sigrid raises her glass to Alasdair and Stefan, with a rousing '*Skål!*'

As she does so, her sleeve falls back, exposing a small tattoo of a raven on her wrist where her watch should be. She notices me noticing and covers it again with her shirt cuff.

When we've finished eating, Stefan fetches a bottle of whisky from his room and gives us each a dram. 'Our only real luxury,' he explains and winks at Sigrid. Stefan's hair is cut very short until he is almost bald. His carefully trimmed beard and moustache emphasise his pouting, salmon-pink lips. His eyes are black pinpricks and as the evening goes on, a deep red flush spreads across his face and his voice grows louder and more insistent.

Talisker wants to talk about the inflatable. How long will it take us to sail to the northern tip of the island?

Sigrid thinks the sea is still too rough. In any case they've been having engine trouble with the boat. Alasdair thinks he needs to order a spare part from the mainland. Better to stay a few more days and see if the weather improves.

The lighting has been turned down to save the generator so I can't make out Talisker's expression, but I detect her exasperated sigh.

'I heard nothing,' Stefan breaks out suddenly, slurring his words. 'I heard no shooting. No doubt your friends will be in touch very soon. You're wasting your time here, Sergeant! You should wait for your boat and go home in the morning. Guests are very welcome, but our little home is rather too small for five. Unless someone would like to share my room, of course.'

Alasdair makes his only contribution to the evening.

'Why don't you shut the fuck up, Stefan,' he says.

Eventually we all go to bed. The study bedroom is small and windowless, and I have a horror of confined spaces. Lying half-dressed on my bunk, unable to relax, I can make out Talisker's voice through the thin wall, still arguing her case with Sigrid.

Eventually I fall into an uneasy doze.

But it's not Stefan's drunken outburst that's keeping me awake.

When I told Dr Nilsson we'd never met before, I knew I was lying.

I recognise her name. I'm familiar with her work, of course.

But where my memory of her should be, there is just a blank, like a missing tooth.

Karen Taylor is a London-based editor and journalist. Her first thriller, *The Trade*, was published by Endeavour Press. Her YA thriller, *Off The Rails*, won a place in the 2016 London Book Fair's Dragons' Den, while a short story, novella and children's book were shortlisted at the Winchester Writers' Festival.

karenlesleytaylor66@gmail.com

Dark Arts

Rocks rained down like a meteorite shower, bouncing off the cliff face, bouncing off Brandon Hammett's face. But he held onto the soggy trainer which squirmed in his hand like a fish, the guy's other foot doing all the damage, kicking sharp pellets and clumps of turf at him.

Brandon could smell blood, feel it slipping down his cheek where one of the stones had made contact. He clamped his mouth shut, didn't want to lose a tooth – didn't want to lose an eye. Was the bloke ever going to give up?

The nutter was halfway up a cliff, fifty feet from certain death on the rocks below, with a copper hanging off his foot.

Where the hell was Philips? He was meant to be at the top, taser ready to wave in the bastard's face if it emerged. The guy's free foot kept on kicking, the other shaking and twisting and then jolted in triumph as it pulled free.

Brandon lunged at the bottom of the man's trousers, the sodden material slipping through his hands. He lunged again, grabbing the ankle beneath, squeezing it hard, making the guy yelp and jerk. The sudden movement threw Brandon off balance and the two of them tumbled onto the wider ledge below.

The guy was on top of him now, one hand forcing his head over the edge. From the corner of his eye Brandon could see the sharp drop, knew he had to flip him. As he heaved himself over, the man grabbed something. *A rock?* The lump of turf smashed down on his face, making him loosen his grip just enough for the guy to pull away. Shaking the dirt from his eyes, Brandon made a grab for a foot, but it kicked away, and he was left with one filthy trainer. He slipped it in his jacket pocket. Could be the sprat to catch his mackerel if this farce ever came to court.

He wiped his sleeve across his eyes, blinking and straining for vision. In the moonlight it was difficult to gauge the guy's age, but he was agile, that's for sure. At thirty-five, Brandon wasn't the fittest cop in town. Winded from the chase, from the climb and the tussle he could only watch as the man scrambled to the top, levered himself up over the edge and sprung to his feet.

Brandon moved to the edge of the ledge and leaned back for a better view. He was legging it now, as lithe as a panther in his black clothes and balaclava. Philips was nowhere to be seen. Menhenrick was after him though, but too far back – she'd never catch him.

'Leave it, Jo,' he called. But she didn't. He knew she wouldn't. And he watched as she pounded the clifftop, her red hair aflame in the light of the moon.

Brandon steadied himself against the cold rock. His hands were covered in blood, not just from the gash to his head, but also from the sharp edges he'd grabbed in his frantic ascent. He was more measured as he felt his way down, taking his time, his feet finding foot holes, his hands reaching for support – a gnarled root, a solid lump of turf – jumping the last few feet onto the sandy beach.

Reaching into his pocket, he pulled out his torch and shone it at the sea. He'd seen something floating in the shallows before taking chase. It didn't look like it was going anywhere fast. The sea was calm, the incoming tide edging its sly delivery into the tiny cove. His small hesitation while he clocked the details could have cost him the race across the beach to the cliff face. Or, perhaps, he should get to the gym more.

Someone called his name and he looked up to see Jo and Philips staring at him. He beckoned them down.

Turning to the three plastic barrels bumping against the rocks, he leaned over, careful not to drench his shoes and trousers, and pulled one onto the sand. There'd been a tip-off about the drop and what was in the barrels – and it wasn't bottles of rum. He turned the stopper, yanked it out and felt inside, pulling out one neat white packet. Making a small incision with his Swiss Army knife, he confirmed his suspicions. Cocaine. There had to be fifty packs in the barrel: worth something on the street. Brandon was lugging the other barrels out of the water when he heard the chatter of Jo and Philips as they dropped down into the cove from the rock steps.

'As expected, boss?' wheezed the plump PC, as he came alongside him.

Brandon gave Philips a long hard look. 'So, where were you? You let our man escape. Although ...' He pulled the trainer from his pocket. 'I may give you the chance to find our Cinderella. Make some door-to-door calls. Have you got an evidence bag on you for this?'

Of course he hadn't.

He shook his head. 'I was in the car park waiting for him to show. There was a transit parked there.' Philips stood idle as Jo took the trainer from Brandon and slipped it into a plastic bag.

'But he didn't show, did he? I take it you've got photos of the van? Made a check on ownership?'

'Yes, boss.'

So not completely useless, then.

'Our man ran off through the fields towards the A30. I put a call through to the station,' Jo said, sealing the evidence bag. 'Told them to get a patrol car out. We could get lucky.'

'Good work, Jo. Looks like someone else's luck ran out this morning, though.' Brandon looked down at the barrels. 'It would have taken a bit of effort to get this cargo delivered. The loss will sting.'

They picked up a barrel each and started to walk back towards the cliff steps.

'Any idea who the grass is?' Jo was looking at him as if he had all the answers.

'Ideas, yes. But not ones I'm on first-name terms with. A ... Nonymous.' Brandon paused. 'Maybe a rival supplier?'

'Why send for us, then?'

'Good question. Perhaps they didn't have the resources to pick this up themselves tonight. Maybe they just wanted to teach someone a lesson. Clear them off their patch.' He stopped walking, readjusted his load. 'Odd that there was just one man – considering there are three barrels. Perhaps someone was tipped off about the tip-off?'

'That would make sense,' Jo said, looking up at him. 'These aren't light.'

Brandon considered the barrel in his arms – figured it may have been dropped at sea and allowed to drift into the cove on the tide. An old smuggler's trick. Or, possibly, the boat was intercepted and the cargo ditched.

He looked up at the sky, saw a few streaks of pink filtering through the black. It was getting light.

'Let's get these tubs back up the steps and into the car.'

Philips drove them the ten miles back to Penzance. The streets were filling up with workers and delivery trucks heading out of town. There were signs of life at the harbour too: fishermen getting ready for the first trawl of the day, rough sleepers rolling up bedding in the bus shelter, a stray sniffing for leftovers in the promenade gardens.

'Wow. They've gone to town this year.' Jo was pointing at a tower of wood on the Quay, the sun rising behind it.

'The Montol bonfire? For the solstice?' Philips said, slowing down to look.

Brandon was impressed. They'd stacked the timber high – fifteen feet or more of it dominated the Quay.

He asked Philips to pull up beside it, so they could get out for a better look. The wood was piled vertically, leaning inwards, a wigwam of timber. There was no security around it. No barriers. The festival organisers never bothered the police – it was a given that people would act responsibly. Brandon smiled – it was what he liked about Penzance, the absence of intrusive health and safety. But he feared for the day when this trust would be abused.

He flinched at the screech of a gull circling above. Thought, for a moment, that it was a siren. But no, too early for that. If their guy had been picked up the patrol car wouldn't be announcing it at 7am.

'Let's get out of here,' he said. But as the others got back in the car, Brandon turned around for another look at the pyre. He rubbed his eyes. The sunrise was messing with its colours, the wood flesh pink in places, dark red in others.

He hadn't been to the Montol for a good few years. Tonight looked like it might be the night to revisit an old tradition.

CHAPTER TWO

Shadows were lengthening in St Mary's Churchyard when the bells chimed four. It was the winter solstice, the shortest day of the year, and Rachel Matthews was sitting on a bench dedicated to someone who had once enjoyed the sea view. She was enjoying it herself, looking down past the neglected headstones and overgrown grass to the wide flagstone promenade which lined the ocean. Waves glowed red and gold in the setting sun.

She didn't turn when she heard footsteps from behind, crunching the frosted grass. St Mary's Churchyard was a popular shortcut from Chapel Street to the Penzance promenade.

The light, quick steps stopped by the bench.

'Thought I might catch you here.' It was Sam Fowler. Or Sam Trenowden since he'd married Julia. He looked down at her through small metal-rimmed glasses, his hands tucked away in the pockets of an expensive-looking coat. There was a pronounced line of intent on the brow below that slicked-back hair.

'You might also have found me at The Hall, Sam,' Rachel replied, glancing up at him and pulling the plastic bag at her side closer.

'Been buying supplies?'

Not waiting for an answer, he sat down beside her.

'I thought this might give us a bit more privacy. A chance to speak openly.'

Rachel turned to look at him. He was sitting, rather theatrically, with his head down, his shiny-gloved hands pressed together between his legs.

'We both know this isn't going to work,' he said, looking back up at her.

Rachel gave him a quizzical stare.

'Things haven't been right since you came to stay. You must know that? Julia's been jumpy. Her son won't speak to me. You rebuff every attempt Julia makes to accommodate you. She got you the job at the school – covered for you to get it.'

'Covered for me?' Rachel cut in. He was speaking quietly, but she was aware his words could carry on the wind. A couple in Montol costumes walked past, the woman giving them a glance.

'You didn't exactly leave your last job on good terms, did you, Rachel?'

Rachel went to stand, tugging at her coat which was trapped beneath his leg.

'How would you know, Sam? Been reading my messages? Is that why I found you in my room the other night? Snooping?'

'No need to get so touchy.' Sam got up to join her. He was barely two inches taller than Rachel and only had to tilt his head to jut a petulant chin in her face.

'We needn't be enemies, Rach,' he said, placing a hand on her arm.

Rachel shook him off and started to walk down the steps towards the stone arch, which led to Under Chapel Yard and the Quay.

'Rachel,' she heard him say, 'there's something I need to discuss with you. It's about the gallery.'

What now? She walked faster, conscious of him scurrying to catch her.

The wind had picked up, blowing her hair across her face. She brushed it aside as Sam moved ahead to block her way. Over his shoulder she could see the waves storming the shore, smashing against the sea wall. Seaweed and froth were being tossed in the air. The scent of the sea mingled with Sam's smell, a musky mix of aftershave and something else, something unpleasant.

'Let's go for a drink. I just want to make a suggestion.' He reached for his phone as it began to ring, raising a palm to stop Rachel moving off.

She looked past him towards St Michael's Mount in the east, the medieval fortress drenched in blood red light. An hour earlier it had been dark as a shadow, rising from the water like some mythical seabird. To the west was the hilly fishing town of Newlyn, its white brick houses stacked like little cartons of fudge.

'Hi, Julia. In Penzance right now,' Sam was saying, 'Yes, they're getting things ready for the Montol. The wood's all stacked up on the Quay, ready for the bonfire. Perhaps we should eat in Chapel Street tonight? Nick? He's coming with us? Thought he'd have some friends of his own age to go with? OK … but he's not a baby any more. OK. I'll text you. B'bye.'

'Shall we go to the Fisherman's Catch?' Sam slipped his phone into his pocket.

Rachel nodded. She was tired after a week at work and a drink would lessen the load which was Sam and his *suggestions*.

He couldn't have picked a better venue for a quiet chat. The Fisherman's Catch was an overrated, over-priced pub, generally avoided by the locals. He steered her to a table in a secluded corner.

'Now, what would you like, young lady?'

Rachel cringed. He was barely a month older than her. She'd known him since she was a young lady. She was thirty-three now and he was still in her life. Living with Julia, meant living with the frenemy too.

'A glass of Cabernet Sauvignon and a crab sandwich, please.'

'A crab sandwich? But we'll be eating later.' Sam's eyes were on the menu and the £15 tab.

'I didn't have any lunch.' Rachel suppressed a smirk. She knew the expense would gall. *Tightwad.*

'Yeah, sure.' Sam got to his feet and headed to the bar, still wearing his coat. He returned with a large glass of red and a small white wine, placing a wooden spoon with a number on it between them.

'They'll be over in a while with your sandwich,' he said, tapping the table with the spoon. 'They're probably out catching it right now – needs to be fresh at that price.' A clipped laugh.

Rachel forced a smile. 'What did you want to discuss?'

'Ah yes,' Sam said, twisting the spoon in one hand. 'Your dad, Rachel. Your dad's paintings. There's a beauty hanging in the Tate at St Ives. I'd like one in the new gallery.'

'I've told you before, I don't have any paintings. Mum doesn't have any either. Dad sold the lot years ago, long before he died. The ones he didn't sell he gave away or traded at the pub. I would like to help. Just can't.'

Sam sighed. 'Rachel, you can do better than that. You must know someone who would loan us a work for the opening? Come on ... you are his daughter. The very talented daughter of the late, great Lawrence Matthews. O. B. bloody E. Matthews. Come on. What about that heiress he was shagging in the nineties? I've heard she's got some. Surely she could loan one?'

'Thanks,' Rachel said, as a young Goth with an elaborate nose ring placed a plate before her.

Sam stared at her, his head cocked to one side, the spoon turning in his hand. 'I wouldn't ask, but ...' He picked a cucumber slice off the small tired salad, resting on her plate.

'I'll try,' Rachel replied, pulling the plate closer and taking a bite of her sandwich.

'That's my Rach.' Sam leaned back in his chair, resting his hands behind his head. 'I know Julia doesn't say anything. She's nuts about you ... we all are. But things have been tense at home. This would be the best possible gesture at this time. Show we are all pulling together. Are on the same canvas.'

Rachel bit into something hard. A piece of shell? As she picked it from her mouth, Sam was back on his feet, walking towards the door, taking a call. She could see him through the window, grinning into his phone, running a gloved hand through his hair. He had his gloves back on. *Pillock.*

'Sorry about that,' he said, plopping back down in his seat, a salacious smile on his face. 'Meghan, from NewlynWave. You know, the small gallery in Newlyn? She came around a few weeks back? Well, she and her bloke Ed are joining us tonight for drinks before the procession.'

Rachel remembered. Meghan was an imposing presence: voluptuous, demonstrative and predatory. If she wasn't actually physically touching you, she'd be sex-raying you from across the room. No wonder Sam was grinning.

His face tightened when his phone buzzed again. Rachel saw a name flick up; someone beginning with B? Sam snapped off the device and put it away.

'No one important,' he said, answering Rachel's look.

Leaning forward he swiped some more salad from her plate and popped it in his mouth.

'You should eat your greens, Rach. You're looking a bit peaky.'

A piece of dark green lettuce was clinging to one of his teeth like seaweed. His feet were tapping under the table. Just stop it, Rachel thought, as she watched him pick up the salt cellar and pour a little hill onto the check cloth.

Swirling a finger in the mound, he said, 'I don't know why you took the job at the school. Julia thought it would be a good idea. But, with all that's happened, I'm not so sure.' He turned to face her.

'I could say it pays the rent. But, thanks to you both, I don't have to pay rent. It ...'

'Fills a void? Kills time?'

'Yep, I guess so.'

Sam downed the last of his wine and got up.

'We're meeting at The Barn at 7pm and then drinks at the Benbow. Weird choice of pub. Haven't been there for years.'

Nor had Rachel. It had featured pretty heavily at one stage, sneaking in on a Friday night for some underage boozing.

She met his eye. 'Going back to The Hall, then?'

'No. Bit of business in town. See you later, Rachel. You'll make that call?'

'Yeah, sure.'

'Sooner rather than later,' he said, flashing a quick, firm smile as he walked away.

Rachel searched for her car keys. She was enjoying the wine, could probably have had another, but she'd promised her mother she would pop in tonight. It was just down the road. It would kill a few hours before it all kicked off for the Montol. Killing hours again. Sam had a point.

CHAPTER THREE

Rachel had spent more hours at her mother's in the past two months than in the past two years. But it still felt strange to walk down the familiar path to Seabird Cottage, the garden just that little bit more forlorn than the time before.

It was almost pitch black as she waited at the front door. Just a few shy stars peeped out of the night sky. She expected her mother to emerge in her usual haze of benign chaos. Streaks of paint on her face, wild greying hair escaping from some sort of scrunch – the last time a pair of skimpy knickers. She was convinced it was a façade. A mask. What disturbed her most was when it slipped.

The mask was intact when she stepped into the ramshackle cottage holding a fraying length of rope from the front door cowbell. Rachel wasn't the most practical person herself, but she was concerned about the state of the place. It was collapsing around them. She put the piece of rope down on the messy living room table.

'Rachel, darling, you don't know your own strength. You don't yank something as fragile as my darling cowbell. You know it's been in the family since ... since Larry and I did Europe. Switzerland – yes that's where we got it. We were staying at this incredibly beautiful house in the country. Belonged to a charming friend of your father's ...' Lizzie Matthews had picked up the rope and was stroking it like a silk scarf.

She'd bought it in a knick-knack shop in Chapel Street back in the '90s, Rachel remembered. One of the many flea market purchases that her mother had made over the years, her daughter tagging behind, repelled by the stale-smelling emporiums, desperate to cut loose.

'Shall I make some tea?' Rachel moved around her towards the kitchen. It wasn't so bad, thank God. Lizzie didn't eat much so the mess was restricted to a few crumb-ridden plates and mismatched tea cups with various liquids lurking at the bottom.

'Not for me, darling. I had one a little while ago. I just want to get on with a portrait I'm working on. Come and see, darling. Leave that.' Lizzie frowned at the dishcloth in Rachel's hand. 'Come and see.'

But I just want to clean up, make supper and get out of here, thought Rachel. She'd brought two ready meals from the Co-op with her. Her visits never went to plan. On the one hand it was brilliant that Lizzie was still painting at seventy-five. On the other, she seemed to be developing a penchant for grotesque Francis Bacon-style portraits. Lizzie had always painted delicate landscapes – since Lawrence died, her paintings had morphed into abstract aberrations.

Rachel braced herself as she followed her mother into the studio. This room, at least, hadn't changed one bit since Lawrence ascended to the great garret in the sky. The smell of turps and oils, the half-filled paint pots with their congealed lids, the massive old wooden table which ran the length of the room, covered in smears and spills, was as it should be. As it always was. There was an easel by the small window at the far end of the room.

'Ta-da!' Lizzie said, arranging her arms like a magician's assistant to frame her creation.

Rachel peered into the gloomy corner at the grim canvas. She could feel her mother's eyes on her. Was that Rachel's green woollen scarf, the one her mother had bought her last Christmas? Probably. A streak of green swirled below a pink oval, framed by an arch of yellow. It wasn't exactly a mirror image; her mother was maxing out her artistic licence. Two dark green pits, circled with red, glared above a sliver of bone and a black gash of a mouth.

Rachel cracked a smile. 'I think you've caught my likeness, but possibly not my *joie de vivre.*'

'Rachel, darling! You like it … it's a departure, I know. But …'

'I know, Mum. Yes, I know.'

Before she could summon the energy to protest, Rachel had been 'styled' and positioned on a stool in the studio. Her foot was tapping like Sam's. She didn't need this. A Radio 4 interviewee was emoting on human rights in the Yemen. Lizzie was frowning and clucking in approval as she mixed paints and angled a lamp, so the light shone straight in Rachel's eyes.

'Mum!'

'Sorry, darling.' Lizzie adjusted the lamp a centimetre.

Rachel glanced up at the clock: 6.15pm. The others would be at The Barn in 45 minutes. Would Sam mention their conversation to Julia? There was no way she was going to find him a painting. Certainly not from that woman. She looked at Lizzie's sweet face creased in concentration. Did she know about her? Probably. She hadn't been her father's first or last lover.

'Mum, how long is this going to take?' Rachel fidgeted on the stool, kicking out her legs like a schoolgirl.

'So, you're rushing off to leave me to go to that tacky Montol carnival.' Lizzie was dabbing at the portrait with a brush. 'Don't move your mouth, darling, I'm working on that sardonic smile of yours.'

'I need to move my lips to answer your question, Mum. Move onto my sardonic brow – add a few more lines.'

'Rachel! Where is the sweet young dreamer that Larry and I knew and loved? Moving to London and working in that ghastly ad agency has made you so brittle.'

Brittle? Broken more like it. But she didn't want to think about it now. The Montol was the first thing she'd looked forward to since arriving back in Penzance. How long would she be expected to stay in town? It was like being trapped in a time-warp emporium. Your mother's going to need you, Doctor Bryant had said. The dementia will develop.

'Dreaming doesn't pay bills, Mum. Anyway, back to the Montol. Yes, I'm going. Haven't been for years. Are people still raiding the junk shops for tatty toff outfits? Have they introduced rap to the usual medieval drone?'

'You'll be disappointed, darling. Move your head to the right, just a little. It's become a commercial jamboree.'

Rachel pulled at the scratchy green wool scarf Lizzie had fixed round her neck. She'd been sitting for nearly 45 minutes. Three electric heaters were whirling away, throwing out heat.

'I thought Market Jew Street looked rather charming. Not commercial at all – lots of little stalls selling local produce.'

'But you bought our supper from the Co-op?'

Grief, does the woman notice everything?

'I don't have time to put a meal together, Mum. This will have to do for tonight. Unless we go to The Barn. Julia is eating there with Sam and Nick. We could join them … if we hurry.'

'No thank you, darling. You go, if you like.' Lizzie put down her paint brush and wiped her hands on her apron.

'I'd rather not. I'll stay here with you and then meet them later for a drink.'

'He was round here earlier, you know.'

'Who?' said Rachel, slipping off the stool and following her mother into the kitchen.

'Slimy Sam.'

'Sam? Whatever for?'

'Oh, some pretence or another. But it didn't take him long to get to the point.'

Rachel sighed. She knew what was coming.

'He was after Larry's paintings. He asked if I had any for the new gallery. I said no and he asked if I was sure. Whether your father hadn't stored some in the attic or wherever. He was very persistent, Rachel. And clueless. Calls himself an art dealer … he must be able to source a Lawrence Matthews. Maybe from one of the London galleries?'

'You would like to think so, wouldn't you? But it would cost him. Sam wants something for nothing as usual. He asked me much the same thing.'

'When?' Lizzie turned away from the sink where she'd been cleaning her palette and brushes.

'This afternoon – he must have left your place and headed straight into Penzance. He found me in St Mary's Churchyard.'

'What were you doing there, Rachel?' Lizzie spoke softly.

'Just having a quiet moment, that's all. It's been a busy week.'

Lizzie walked across the red-tiled floor and rested a hand on Rachel's arm. 'You go and sit down for a little while, darling. Let me sort supper.'

'I've been sitting down for nearly an hour.'

'But we all know that sitting for an artist is not like sitting, sitting. And it's only ping ping carbonara. Off you go – there's *Tate Magazine* on the coffee table, I think. Your father's in it.'

Rachel found the magazine poking out from under the sofa. It fell open at page six. The painting wasn't one of his best, but they'd positioned it well in the light-filled reception. The *Head of The Titan* would make an imposing first impression. As Lawrence Matthews always had. Charming people and frightening them in equal measures, he could as well have been an actor as an artist, thought Rachel. His public life was performance art. But beneath the bravado, there was real talent, raw emotion. The best times were sitting in the studio, chatting over the radio, watching him paint. He put painstaking care and precision into those trademark torrents of colour; standing back, retouching, asking her opinion. There was mutual respect between artist and artist, father and daughter. And love. She sometimes forgot about the love.

Lizzie brought trays in and they sat in front of the TV, Lizzie toying with strips of tagliatelle. She dropped her fork on her plate and pushed it away. 'Got anything to wear tonight? You can't go like that.'

'It will have to do.'

Lizzie screwed up her nose. 'I'll find you something. You will be the belle of the ball – not a dreary schoolmarm. I'll just go and see what I can find in my witchy-poo wardrobe.'

Rachel had washed the dishes and vacuumed by the time Lizzie returned with satin and velvet garments thrown over one skinny arm. She was wearing a big floppy felt hat.

'You should come too, Mum.' Rachel swooped on the clothes. She remembered them well from Larry and Lizzie's glory days.

'These are perfect. Just the right amount of dust and moth holes for Montol authenticity.'

Lizzie smiled indulgently as Rachel sorted through the clothes.

'You should wear the red velvet.' Lizzie caressed the rich fabric, breathed in the scent of yesterday's parties. 'It's Biba.'

'It's beautiful.' Rachel slipped it on. She'd lost weight and the Twiggy-size '70s dress fitted, just about.

'And the hat. You can't go to the Montol without a hat ... and scarf.'

Rachel took the purple felt hat and the woollen green scarf, which, although incongruous, suited the crazy dress code.

'You look lovely, darling,' Lizzie said as she stood in the porch to see her off.

'Sure you don't want to come, Mum?'

'No, darling. I've been to enough spooky solstice celebrations. I prefer to stay at home with my own demons. They're company enough.'

Wendy Turbin works in education and studied creative writing with the OU for her bachelor's degree. She once won a *Writers' News* competition and has since had stories published in print and online. *Sleeping Dogs* is her debut novel, reflecting her love of the supernatural and private detective fiction.

wendyturbin@gmail.com

Sleeping Dogs

Thanks to the bite of the North Sea easterly, I drove the short distance from my office to the other side of Haston to reach Emily Dunker's comfortable semi. This meant I could wear my smartest, though not warmest, coat and arrive with my curls in a neat-ish ponytail instead of a birds' nest tangle.

I wondered why Mrs Dunker needed a private detective. Whatever she wanted, I hoped it would pay enough to shore up my finances for another week or two.

Emily answered the door almost immediately and directed me into what my paternal grandmother would have called the front parlour. I guessed she had been watching out for me from behind the nets. She was a scarecrow of a woman, straw-haired, thin-lipped, in her mid-thirties. She could have been younger. Her careworn, worried air did little to enhance her looks.

Pot and kettle, Penny-lope?

The comment, an echo of my father's voice from before his fatal heart attack, found its mark. No one would describe my look as polished and my own troubles were carving grooves round my mouth.

'Would you like a cup of tea?'

I shook my head. She seemed anxious to put off the moment when she had to give away her secrets and raised her voice from a mumble to a whisper.

'Are you sure? There's cake too. It should be home-made but ...' Her explanation died beneath the world's weight on her shoulders.

My instinct was to gather the essential facts and move swiftly on, earning the cash being my priority, but Dad had always said rapport encourages 'the punters' to sign up. He claimed the more they trust you, the more they'll pay.

I wasn't in his league when it came to charming clients, but I did my best and tried to be upfront about the cost.

Cranking out a smile, I nodded my thanks. I resigned myself to staying until the Tetley's cooled and teacake had been crumbled, even if I couldn't solve her problem. She bustled off to put the kettle on.

The postponement gave me time to snoop, one of my favourite hobbies, and to have a closer look at the ghost.

She was twelve or thereabouts, skinny-legged in jodhpur jeans, wide-eyed and worried. Soft toys and lettered cubes piled in one corner were faintly visible through her boots. The bruises on her arms, dark shadows below her short T-shirt sleeves, were the most solid thing about her. Big thumbprints stood out clearly.

I wondered when she died and why she was still here. For now, she seemed content to watch.

I turned to investigate the alcove by the fireplace and was pleased to source the tinny notes that had been, almost subliminally, annoying me. In the dusty depths there lurked a baby monitor, now silent. Above the clatter of crockery from the kitchen, a floorboard creaked overhead, then the nursery tune started up again.

I guessed that at the other end was one of those mobiles that amuse the young as they wait for the sandman. A sleepy chuckle supported this idea.

On the same shelf stood a charity calendar, with photogenic lifeboat men leaning against gunwales looking faintly embarrassed. February's crew gave off a strong vibe of 'my wife said I had to'. These volunteers did a great job as I should know. I owed them my life. The bare manly chests didn't spoil the view either.

Next to this, a framed swimming certificate for Jasmina Dunker, aged 11, was paired with a school photo of a chubby girl with a blunt fringe. The image was slightly blurred as if she couldn't stay still long enough to be captured by the camera.

The fake log fire which might have made the room feel cheery was dark and lifeless. The radiators clunked and gargled then stopped. I hoped it would remain toasty in view of the sub-zero temperature outside. Emily broke the silence, returning in a flurry of plates, cups and coasters.

We settled, the small table between us bearing the results of her labours. Emily Dunker couldn't put it off much longer though I suspect she tried. Her gaze strayed around the room, sliding over the heap of baby clothes, clean but not folded, on the back of the chair and, on the wall above, their wedding photograph. Smiles and confetti preserved forever behind heart-shaped glass.

Her eyes finally came to rest on me. I heard the ting-a-ling as if the gentle breeze of an open window had started the mobile up again. The silence between us grew uncomfortable. It might have lasted forever if I hadn't broken it. I cleared my throat.

'Well, Mrs Dunker, what can Wiseman Associates do for you?'

'My husband – he mustn't know I've called you.' Her voice was low, and she looked around as if the words would hover in the air for him to read on his return. 'He'd be so mad at me.'

'OK.' I was hopeful. Infidelity was sometimes a grubby gig, but it played to our strengths – observe, photograph, report – and netted a reliable income. I hastily assured her that confidentiality was guaranteed.

Emily swallowed hard, then picked up her cup. She sipped, rattled it down in the saucer, opened her mouth a time or two and licked her thin, cracked lips. Finally, she told me what was on her mind, peeping through lowered lashes like a poor man's Lady Di.

'My Brian's a good man,' she started. 'A good husband and father.'

Of course he is, chipped in my mean internal voice, that's why you need a private detective.

'He travels for his job sometimes, and I'm not naive, I know these things happen. He's very good looking so I can understand he'd attract someone, and since the baby came along it's been so hard for him.'

And it's a breeze for you, I thought, a picnic in the park.

'He's been through it all before, you see, the nappies and sleepless nights and everything. And Jasmina's a credit to him – a joy to both of us – I didn't think I could get pregnant so when I did, well, it seemed like it was fate, you know? To have a child together and complete the family,' she said.

I nodded though I wondered if Jasmina was quite so pleased to have a sibling vying for her father's attention. My own sister had sometimes felt like a cuckoo in the nest, and there were only five years between us.

Emily was picking up the pace now and out it came in a rush – the distance she felt, Brian's distraction when he was home, going out with unnamed 'friends' more often.

'Then he said he was rehearsing on Friday night,' she hesitated, blinking fast. 'I bumped into their play's director in Tesco and he was hopping mad because they'd had to cancel – the hall was double-booked.'

'Rehearsing?'

'Nonsense really, amateur stuff, but Brian's done it for years and I suppose other men go to football or something.' She waved that away. 'He lied though. And lately he's been acting strange – not sleeping properly and going for walks early in the morning when he's always loved his lie-in.' She took a jerky breath, then continued more quietly. 'Then there was the letter – he looked so angry when it came. He said it was nothing, just a mistake. I heard him put it in his desk.'

She responded to my raised eyebrow. 'The top drawer sticks, and he banged it and swore – that's not like him – and then he stormed out.'

Her cup was gripped between her hands and I hoped it was more robust than it looked as she reached the heart of her suspicion.

'I searched, and he must have taken the envelope with him only ...' Her head came up and she looked me in the eye. 'Right down the back where he keeps his passport and that – I found this.' She handed it over like a woman doing her duty under fire. 'I think he's being blackmailed.'

The glossy photo showed the man in their wedding picture sprawled on a rumpled bed, eyes closed, mouth open – it implied the aftermath of too much booze and illicit sex. A twisted sheet failed to disguise a lightly furred pot-belly but was placed, by luck or design, over the parts other beers can't reach. I was grateful.

The smeared red stain across his mouth said the lipstick of this 'blackmailer' was the same colour as her underwear – the shiny push-up bra discarded beside him. She was a well-built girl if this item was to be believed.

His five o'clock shadow was way past midnight, his hair mussed into a dark coxcomb and his jaw line was blurring. The image had the seedy look of a tired D-lister doing soft porn to pay the rent.

I turned the photo over and written on the back in a loopy hand it said, 'Great night! Let's do it again soon, Honey.' Someone had left a kiss underneath, and the pale pink lips seemed to smile mockingly.

The whole thing felt like a set-up, or a practical joke, and why would Brian Dunker leave this photo in his desk but take the envelope away?

Incredulity pulled the inside of my mouth like lemon juice.

But if it was a joke, his wife wasn't laughing. She was on the edge of tears.

'It doesn't prove anything, Emily,' I said, 'not even a one-night stand. Maybe a stag-night gag on a man who likes a drink or four?'

'He's been drawing out money – two thousand over the last six weeks and never said a word to me – and he's ever so stressed.' She blinked at the rich fruit loaf she'd brought in with the tea. 'He's not even eating properly.'

Her anguish was so real that I resisted pointing out he could do with losing a few pounds.

Pot and kettle, again, Pen.

I sucked in my stomach and gave up thoughts of a second slice.

Emily hurried on. 'You'll think I'm a fool, but I love him and whatever he's done he doesn't deserve to be so unhappy. I just want my Brian back; back the way he used to be.' She started to cry, big fat drops spilling over and dripping off her chin.

While she reached for the tissues, I turned away and tried not to feel Jasmina's bright face beaming down at me from the shelf.

Tears were understandable, but weeping was getting us nowhere. I stifled the urge to ask why she didn't just tell him that she knew. Maybe he was waiting for the final push, the big fight scene, to leave her behind.

Still, something else was off. I was certain someone was lurking upstairs, soothing the child, resetting that mobile and listening to every word on the baby monitor.

And then there was my ghost.

Spirits, apparitions, revenants – whatever you want to call them – most focus on their own activities but this one had drifted closer and turned her empty eyes on me. She floated just above the carpet, head on one side as if considering, then she reached out. There was a deep aching chill, as if an icicle was held against my cheek, then she faded slowly into nothing.

Emily had mopped her eyes and when I tuned back in, she was expanding on a phone call she had overheard.

'He's arranged to meet someone at the end of the pier on Saturday. He said he'd bring the money.' Her eyes skimmed past the baby monitor, giving me a fair idea of how she'd garnered that nugget. 'You've got to find out who it is and tell her to leave him alone.'

I'd been spun an unlikely yarn, but beggars can't be choosers and my skin still felt the ghost girl's touch.

Emily signed the standard contract with hardly a glance at the fine print, and I agreed to do my best.

Leaving Emily clearing up in what seemed an atypical fit of tidiness, I climbed into my trusty Fiesta and drove around the corner. Once parked, I changed my red wool coat for a grey Puffa and pulled a beanie low on my forehead. I strolled back, hunching my shoulders against the cold.

Pausing on Carlton Drive, changing the cartridge in my e-cig and sucking steam into my lungs, I glanced in at the Dunkers' front window. Sure enough, a man's broad-shouldered figure was silhouetted against the nets, his back to me. The lamp lit the room like a stage set but Emily bustled in and twitched the curtains shut.

I was considering how long I could loiter on the off-chance he'd emerge when my skinny spirit appeared shimmering on the Dunkers' driveway.

She drifted closer, pointed to my feet where a small tabby, kerbstone visible through its body, was trying to wind itself around my ankles. She giggled soundlessly as it passed right through me. I shuddered but the cat seemed fatalistic, busying itself grooming its stripes. When in doubt, wash, says the feline code and this seemed to hold good even after death, but my doubts needed more productive action. I put the e-cig away, stuck my cold hands in my pockets and headed back to my car.

CHAPTER TWO

In the distance, the reflection of Haston's pleasure pier shimmered on the North Sea tide. Gulls huddled on cold shingle to the east of the town where, a few streets inland, a glow from an attic window diffused into the night sky.

Underneath the lights, in her workroom, Alice leaned over her sewing machine as it whirred against the backdrop of soft TV voices. She guided the seam beneath the foot, and it emerged neatly joined, a cascade of satin and tulle.

The dress rehearsal was fast approaching, and she had to get Titania's dress finished tonight. Unlike her usual clients, these actors were amateur, but the dramatics would be worthy of Hollywood royalty if everything wasn't ready.

The players took themselves so very seriously, and none more so than director Terence – 'not Terry, if you please' – who had begged Alice to help them out. Their usual wardrobe mistress had deserted, and Alice couldn't blame her. The East Coast of England was no match for sunny Tenerife, especially when the low cloud rolled in. It had barely been daylight for weeks.

The doorbell, emphasised by Montie's warning bark, disturbed her musing. Like a devil summoned by her thoughts, Terence materialised on her front step.

'Just popped in while passing,' he announced breezily, 'see how you're getting on.' Alice had little doubt he was also hoping to run into one of the professional performers whose rent enabled her to pay the bills. If any of her lodgers found fame, Terence would be in name-dropping heaven.

This evening he was out of luck. The only residents at home were herself and Montie. The Basset, naturally, greeted the visitor with great enthusiasm. Terence came armed with treats and Montie was beginning to develop a certain roundness.

Alice sighed and offered tea.

'I just wish doggie chocs could make us all so happy,' Terence began when they were seated. 'Honestly, I'm at my wits' end. Not only did I have to cancel the run-through on Friday, but I've got Helena disrupting our evenings.' He raised one eyebrow. 'I thought it was called *morning* sickness, darling, and God knows who the father is. I'm sure she doesn't.'

He waited, taking a sip from his cup, but Alice kept silent. She would not add fuel to the old gossip's fire. He pursed his lips.

'And what's going on with Brian? He's usually one of my best, but his Demetrius is all over the place, missing cues, messing up his lines.' He sipped his tea again, regarding her over the rim. 'He seems to have developed a bit of a thing for you, darling, hardly took his eyes off you in rehearsal yesterday, and you were having quite the cosy chat in the car park before we left. Care to share?'

No, thought Alice. Absolutely not, or it would be all around the town in a nanosecond and if it got back to Emily there would be fireworks to rival Guy Fawkes. The Basset provided inspiration.

'Brian just wants me to cut his costume to hide the paunch a bit. He asked me to be discreet.'

Terence snickered. 'We all have our little vanities, and he had been getting porky though I rather thought he'd become quite svelte of late. Of course, he'd be wasting his time with you, darling, wouldn't he, unless you're thinking of switching sides?'

He smirked, making Alice wonder who on earth he'd been talking to now. She made no secret of being gay, but she didn't broadcast her private life on an open channel either.

Ignoring Montie, who nosed his arm hopefully, Terence went on.

'Well, it's obvious Brian's carrying a torch, my dear, and him a married man. Tut, tut.' Terence prattled on while Alice wondered what he'd say if he had any idea how far he was from the truth. Brian had sworn her to secrecy about his plans practically on pain of death and, though Alice disliked the subterfuge, the customer was always right.

Terence's focus had returned to the company's upcoming production.

'Thank the lord the costumes are under control.' He paused briefly to peer over his specs. 'They are under control, Alice, aren't they?'

'They'll be fine, Terence, but only if I can get on, so if you don't mind ...' She continued to reassure him as she ushered him to the door, but he wasn't quite finished.

'You will just alter Helena's dress – let it out a bit, won't you? I could drop it round,' he offered.

'No, Terence. Sorry. I've too much to do already. Someone else will have to do it,' she said, and bit down on the reminder that she had a living to earn with real paying clients with deadlines whose dresses wouldn't make themselves.

He drew his mouth down at the corners and steepled his hands in a theatrical plea, but she remained unmoved. With her father's imminent arrival in town, she'd have one drama queen to indulge soon enough. She wasn't about to start encouraging another.

'Oh well, if Helena splits her seams on stage the *Gazette*'s critic might give us a better review – old lech that he is.'

Takes one to know one, thought Alice, shutting the door firmly.

She was smoothing Titania's finished garment as *News at Ten* came on. Cued by the theme tune, Montie pawed at the door. She let him into the back garden, rolling her eyes at his smug expression as he trotted past and snuffled off into the shadows.

The outdoor light had failed to come on. She added replacing the bulb for the second time this month to her growing mental to-do list as she hurried back upstairs.

Montie would bark when he wanted to come in, followed by an unearthly howl if he wasn't promptly attended to. The neighbours, already touchy about her lodgers' late-night lifestyle and occasional flamboyant outfits, were only too ready to complain about the noise. Hopefully she'd have five minutes to tidy up her workroom before Montie's summons sounded.

A few minutes later, Alice returned the last reel of thread to its place and turned off the TV. The clock chimed the quarter. Silence from below.

She frowned.

Once, in the early days, Montie had managed to escape, but Alice had replaced the old fence and checked the new one regularly. Even so, a stirring of concern was beginning to make her fingertips itch.

She started down the stairs. He wouldn't come in before he was ready even if she called – Montie could give a mule lessons in stubborn – but she could shine a light on whatever he was up to. Digging up old bones in the shrubby wilderness at the top end of the garden probably. Still, he was never out this long at night. Could he have dug his way out? She hurried into the kitchen.

Naturally, the torch batteries were dead and, beyond the patch of light spilling from the back door, all was black. Alice peered into the darkness.

It was useless.

She was dithering between rattling the treats bag which sometimes brought the greedy hound running or dashing upstairs for the light on her phone, when the front doorbell rang. It was swiftly followed by a loud rapping. Alice's heart quickened as she flew to answer. No one knocked like that without reason.

A woman turned away as the door opened. Alice heard, 'dog lying in the gutter', but as the stranger waved towards the road and babbled on about a thud and a car speeding away, Alice absorbed almost nothing.

Montie!

A few words did follow Alice as she fled down the path, pulsing red in her mind like neon. 'He's unconscious or dead.'

Unconscious, she begged, throwing herself on her knees beside him. Please, please, let him be unconscious.

As the woman accelerated Alice's car through the empty streets, Alice prayed for Montie to wake. His head lolled, his heavy body swaying with the car's movement, soft and unresisting. She could see no blood, but Alice coaxed the mud from his shoulder with feather touches, fearing what damage could be hidden beneath his smooth, warm fur. She greeted each rise of his chest with relief, whispering, 'Hold on, Montie. Hold on,' then held her own breath till he took his next.

An eternity later the car swung into the parking place on the far side of the building where the vet and his nurse were waiting. Dan Kitson was one of the best, Alice told herself as Montie was transferred onto a trolley and wheeled away towards the operating theatre.

Alice kept pace until her way was barred with an apologetic gesture from the nurse and she was directed into the waiting room.

It was only then she realised the stranger who had helped so much had disappeared into the night. She didn't even know her Good Samaritan's name.

She'd find the woman later, she resolved, and thank her properly. For now, her thoughts were centred on the waiting room door and the surgery beyond.

Montie's life was in Dan Kitson's hands. All Alice could do now was wait.

My trainee-cum-receptionist jerked his chin in greeting as I walked past into my office. Dad's view had been that the agency's clients should be met with confident efficiency from the start. He'd been fulsome in praise of his assistant, Maggie Holt. Sadly, she had chosen to retire, and such people were paid a lot more than I could offer. I made do with her nephew, Nathan.

Nate did his best. He even pushed the chewing gum to one side of his cheek as he agreed an appointment time with whoever was on the phone. New business, hopefully.

I'd been out trying to stay alert while nothing much happened on an insurance case. It was late in the day before I'd hit the jackpot, but the final footage of the 'incapacitated' claimant playing tennis meant the client would be pleased.

Now I updated the job log, uploaded the video, and set an action for Nate to email the invoice tomorrow. The income would look good at the creditors' meeting – if that's what it came to.

A glance at my naked wrist where my father's Seamaster watch used to be did not improve my spirits. I'd have to break that habit along with the smoking I could no longer afford.

A moment later Nate was leaning against my office doorway. I waved him in.

'I've put a Mr Haddock in for Thursday at three,' he said. 'About his wife's yoga instructor, something fishy apparently.'

'He never said that!'

'He did.' Nate grinned. 'Dunno how I kept it together. I put it in the book for Robbie to do the initial consult. He could do with a laugh. You're showing as unavailable, but no details?'

'Fine, Nate. Thanks.' I declined to enlighten him about my scheduled meeting with the bank.

'Coffee?' he asked.

'No, don't bother. You get off home. I'll hold the fort for the last hour.'

I heard him whistling down the stairs a few minutes later. Oh, to be young and carefree. I'd settle for either one right now.

Pushing the hair out of my eyes, I set to work on my new case.

Time sped by as I consolidated what I'd already gleaned about the Dunkers via the internet and added new details, then I reviewed the results.

The Dunkers' credit rating was reasonable, they had no criminal convictions and their public social media presence was limited. They were both registered to vote, could drive and had no outstanding speeding tickets or fines.

Such solid citizens were good news for me. There was a chance of getting paid and, though they didn't own the semi in Carlton Drive, they had been renting for a while and seemed unlikely to flit.

A little more trawling brought up random details. The *Gazette* billed Brian as a leading light of the Haston Amateur Dramatic Society, and he was on a quiz team in the local league; Emily had been a teaching assistant at Haston High, pictured smiling prettily with a bouquet and a baby bump – presumably now on maternity leave – and had helped run the hospice fete. I noted that, in addition to her swimming, Jasmina had taken a minor role in a school musical. There was a picture of her taking a bow. An Oscar winner couldn't have smiled any wider.

No other child was mentioned though, no deceased sibling or other teenaged Dunker anywhere so nothing that raised red flags as far as my ghost girl was concerned. I had to figure she was not a Dunker. I needed a name.

The owners of the Dunkers' house were listed as Barbara and John Nash. If my sad spirit was connected to them, I'd have to dig deeper – but the cold touch on my face had faded and ghost research wouldn't pay the bills. The dead would have to wait.

Emily had said her husband worked at Kendall's Textiles – but she'd proved him a liar, so it was worth a check. Their website showed Brian as a current employee and runner-up for 'Salesperson of the Year' two years ago. The photo showed the man with the lightly furred pot-belly in a rather trimmer incarnation being presented with his award. Perhaps success had gone to his stomach. Or failure to win had sent him comfort eating.

Thinking of eating, I had an appointment with a microwave curry and two episodes of the compulsive but implausible *Silent Witness*. They'd probably both give me indigestion, but we all have our vices. My stomach rumbled. Time to go home.

Fortunately for my hunger pangs the office was also where I now lived. Above it to be precise, in a tiny bedsit.

I was just locking the office door when my sister arrived, not even slightly out of breath after running up the stairs to the agency. I hadn't told her of my change of abode, so she followed me up the next flight in silent puzzlement. The silence was short-lived.

An estate agent might have called my new residence 'bijou' but 'not big enough to swing a cat' was Sarah's verdict. I put down the alarm clock I was forced to rescue as she twirled a pillow from my bed to demonstrate.

'I don't plan to take up cat swinging, the housework is super-fast, and I can make tea without leaving my bed.'

She ignored me, of course.

'What happened to that lovely apartment you had? Such a great sea view, you loved it there.'

'They put a wind farm on the sandbank, so I moved out.' I knew it sounded weak. The wind farm was an irritation, a minor blot on the seascape, and the view was still great.

It didn't take her long to start a new thread when she noticed, a moment later, that my left wrist was bare.

'Oh, Pen. Dad's Seamaster, you haven't lost it?' Her voice was tight with distress.

'Of course not!'

I treasured that watch almost as much as Dad had done. He was given it by one very grateful client back in 2002. It was the sort of watch that was designed to last, to hand down from generation to generation and when he'd told me it would be mine one day he'd said, 'I hope you'll pass it on to your own child one day – though finding the right man would be a start.' Then he'd laughed and added, 'Just look after it, Pen.'

My sister assessed the evidence against me, while Dad's words weighed heavy on my conscience.

'You sold it!' she accused.

'I haven't lost it and I didn't sell it,' I said, more to reassure myself than her.

Sarah's fists unclenched then clenched again as I muttered, 'I hocked it.'

She started slow and quiet and just a little bit incredulous, but I could see her working up a lather. 'You pawned Dad's watch?'

She got louder, starting to huff like a winded horse through that long Wiseman nose as she went on. 'You pawned it, Pen?'

I shook my head, not denying, just too filled with failure to explain.

She narrowed her eyes and I could see she was considering how much I'd always treasured that watch. Then my bossy little sister turned into our mother.

'Penelope Wiseman, you had better tell me exactly what's been going on.'

Bridget Walsh left teaching to pursue her love of writing. Her PhD on Victorian murder grew out of her interest in crime fiction and the nineteenth century. She is the recipient of the 2019 David Higham Crime Fiction Scholarship. Bridget lives in Norwich with her husband and two dogs.

bridgetwalsh94@gmail.com

The Stanhope Venus

CHAPTER ONE

Minnie Ward shucked the last of her oysters and drained her beer glass. Cora Monroe, a young woman in a gentleman's suit, leaned over Minnie's shoulder to look in the dressing-room mirror, tucking a few strands of dark hair under her top hat. Further down the corridor of the music hall, bursts of laughter and conversation flared out as other dressing-room doors opened and then slammed shut. An operatic soprano struggled its way up and down a scale, failing to find most of the notes.

Minnie winced.

'Pick a key, Selina,' she murmured. 'Any key.'

'Wouldn't make no difference,' Cora said. 'She'd still sound like a cat pissing in a tin.'

Cora rose and closed the door, then nudged Minnie out of the way and seated herself in front of the mirror. She finished applying her make-up, her tongue peeping between her lips with concentration. When she was done, she pushed a copy of *The Illustrated London News* over to Minnie, past the pots of greasepaint, other stage make-up and dirty rags littering the table.

'Here,' Cora said, tapping her finger at an article, 'what d'you reckon? Wouldn't mind him investigating me.'

Minnie glanced at the pencil sketch of a man wearing an evening suit, top hat and monocle. The headline blazoned: 'Albert Easterbrook: Champion of the Working Classes.' She scanned the article. A gentleman detective whose mission was to 'help those who cannot help themselves' had tracked down a pickpocket targeting the elderly. The pickpocket was also sketched for the reader, a grisly-looking individual closer to a bear than a man.

Minnie snorted.

'Not your type?' Cora asked. 'Pickiness won't win prizes, my girl.'

'I ain't after any prizes. Although I do wonder what he does with the monocle when – you know.'

Cora lifted one quizzical eyebrow. 'You, Miss Ward, are a very saucy girl, and not the kind of young lady a Champion of the Working Classes would want to be courting. Me, on the other hand ...'

Minnie pushed the paper to one side and eyed the ha'penny bun on the table in front of her. Cora followed her gaze and smiled. Every Saturday Minnie bought a cake to be shared later with her family. Most Saturdays the cake never made it home.

'Here, Monroe,' Minnie said, adopting an aristocratic tone and mournfully handing over the cake, 'remove this delicious confection from my sight.'

Cora placed the cake in a drawer and locked it, throwing the key in amongst the pots and bottles on top of the table.

'Hardly seems worth it, Min,' she said. 'You'll be out of here in a few minutes, won't you?'

'Should be.'

As if her anticipation of leaving the music hall had summoned him forth, like an unhelpful genie in a bottle, she heard her name being called. The voice drew closer until, without even the briefest of knocks, the dressing-room door burst open. A diminutive man – no one dared call him short – sporting a brown velvet suit and an elaborate set of whiskers, stood in the doorway. Mr Edward Tansford, owner of the Variety Palace Music Hall. Known as Tansie by everyone, although only a select few were afforded the privilege of calling him that to his face. Minnie was one of the few.

'She ain't here,' Tansie bellowed.

'If you're looking for a mind reader you've come to the wrong door,' Minnie said. 'Who are we talking about?'

'Rose. She's on the missing list.' Tansie turned to Cora and shouted, 'You seen her?'

Cora shook her head and made a show of completing her already finished make-up.

Minnie frowned. 'That's not like Rose.'

Rose Watkins was a regular performer at the Variety Palace. A tightrope walker and acrobat, she was billed as 'The Angel of the Air'.

'Well, it's like her tonight,' Tansie said.

'You asked Billy?'

'Can't find him neither. He's meant to be on the doors in thirty minutes, and he's nowhere.'

'Checked the bar?' Minnie asked.

'No, I ain't checked the bar. I'm the bleeding proprietor of this establishment, Minnie, not some backstage runner.'

'I could have a look?' Minnie offered.

'Yes, you could, couldn't you? Quick smart.'

Minnie bridled. 'I think the phrase you're looking for is, "Thank you so much for offering to help".'

'Just find her, Min,' Tansie growled.

Minnie left the dressing room, navigating her way through the cramped backstage corridors. Cigar smoke caught in her throat, its dusty odour mingling with the smell of greasepaint and cheap perfume. Passing one of the dressing rooms she heard breaking crockery, followed by quiet sobbing. The card pinned on the door said *Betty Gilbert, Plate Spinner.* Her first night. Clearly, rehearsals weren't going to plan. Minnie made a mental note to check on her after she'd spoken to Billy and wondered if she'd ever get home in time for supper.

She came out onto the stage where the piano waited for Selina, the unfortunate soprano. Facing the row of unlit footlights Minnie was reminded of her days as a performer, the hundreds of pairs of eyes on her. Her stomach turned, and she hurried off the stage.

The lamplighters were at work. Hundreds of gas burners around the auditorium were being coaxed into life, lighting Minnie's way as she wove through the groups of tables towards the mahogany bar at the front of the auditorium. There were doors to four snuggeries behind the bar. Minnie tried the first two with no luck, before opening the third to find Billy Walker lolling on a sofa upholstered in vivid pink.

Billy leapt up as the door opened, almost dropping his pipe. Seeing Minnie, he relaxed back onto the couch. He was tall, well-built, as a chucker-out needed to be. He made an impressive sight, with dark hooded eyes and biceps the size of a man's thigh. Minnie knew Billy's type all too well. She had tried warning Rose when he had first started sniffing around.

'But he's so lovely to look at, Min,' Rose had said. 'Those eyes! And his forearms!'

Yes, and those fists, Minnie had thought.

'Well, ain't you quite the don,' Minnie said, pushing Billy's feet off and perching on the end of the couch. 'Wait until Tansie catches you in here. You'll be for it.'

Billy shrugged and continued smoking his pipe.

'Rose is on the missing list,' Minnie said. 'You seen her?'

Billy shook his head. 'Not since this morning. She was on her way out. Wouldn't say where.'

Minnie thought for a moment. 'What was she wearing?'

'What's that got to do with anything?'

'Might give us a clue where she was going.'

'I dunno,' Billy shrugged. 'Clothes. She was wearing those shoes.'

'The new ones?'

'Yeah. She must think me a proper muff. We had an exchange of language, and I ain't seen her since.'

The Variety Palace was used to hearing Rose and Billy argue, but their most recent one had been the worst. Billy had found an expensive pair of cream silk shoes, embroidered with tiny roses, in her dressing room. They would have cost several weeks' wages, and Rose wouldn't reveal how she'd come by the money. Billy had jumped to the obvious conclusion. Minnie couldn't say she blamed him.

'And you've got no idea where she might be?' Minnie asked.

'None. When you find her, tell her to stay out of my way. I've got a liking to make it a little warm for Miss Rose Watkins.' He knocked out his pipe on the snuggery floor and left the room, slamming the door behind him.

Minnie retrieved the remains of the tobacco from the floor. She had no great fondness for Billy but, if he lost his job, Rose might be the one to suffer.

As she made her way back to the dressing rooms, the auditorium was slowly coming to life. The gilt-framed mirrors lining the walls reflected back the dozen waiters in dark suits and white aprons, checking the tablecloths were all hanging at the same length. Tansie was a stickler for detail.

Reaching the backstage area, she followed his bellowing.

'Well?' he said. 'Did you find her?'

Minnie shook her head. 'Billy ain't seen her since this morning.'

Tansie swore.

'I could nip round?' Minnie offered. 'There and back in twenty minutes.'

'No. I need you here. You're my right hand, Min. I'm gonna have to change the running order, and that'll set them all off.'

'I'm a writer, Tanse, remember?' Minnie said. 'Songs and sketches, that's me. If you want me here every night to keep the girls calm, you need to pay me for my time.'

Tansie and Minnie had this discussion at least once a week. Invariably, it ended with Minnie agreeing to stay, although vowing it would be the last time.

'I'm in trouble here, Min,' Tansie said. 'The girls don't listen to me the way they do you.'

'Well, at least send a lad round to her house. It's Rose, Tansie. She's worked here for years and she's never once been late. Send a lad.'

Tansie frowned, then nodded. He fished in his pockets and extracted a ha'penny. 'Give him a flatch,' he said, handing Minnie the single coin, 'but only once he's back, mind.'

Minnie walked to the stage door, where a group of young lads were loitering as they did every night, hoping for some scrap of work. She picked Bobby, the smallest of the boys who looked no more than five or six but was probably twice that age.

'14 Wych Street,' she said. 'Ask if they've seen Rose. Then come straight back with the answer, you hear me? There's something in it for you, but only if you're quick.'

At the suggestion of a reward, Bobby sped off. Minnie turned back into the music hall and was accosted almost immediately by Tansie. He eyed her speculatively.

'You're looking at me like I'm the canary and you're the cat that ain't been fed for a week,' Minnie said.

'I couldn't persuade you? Your old act?'

Minnie took a deep breath. 'We have had this conversation many times, Tanse. Nothing will make me get up in front of those lights again.'

'But you were the best mimic I ever saw, Min. And a face just made for comedy.'

'Thanks, Tanse. Just what a girl wants to hear.'

'You know what I mean. Your face moves around a lot.'

'Seriously, this much sweet talk could kill me. I ain't doing it.'

'Well, I've got a twenty-minute turn and no one to fill it.'

'Can't you get anyone to stretch it out a bit?'

'Already tried. If the dog and monkey act are on stage any longer than twenty minutes the dog'll eat the monkey. Or maybe it's the monkey who'll eat the dog. Either way, bloodshed. The Mexican Boneless Wonder is already as drunk as a boiled owl, and it'll be a miracle if he makes it to the end of his act. And the one-legged dancer muttered something unmentionable when I asked her.'

Minnie arched an eyebrow. 'Selina's always keen.'

'I must have been off me chump the day I hired her,' Tansie said, a look of genuine sadness on his face. 'But if there's no one else—'

'Problems, dear boy?'

The voice was rich and syrupy, every vowel stretched to its limits. Bernard Reynolds, a theatre veteran who had once specialised in Shakespearean monologues but was now only ever given 'thinking parts'. He wore his remaining strands of hair combed over his bald head, fixed with a pomade of his own recipe, made primarily from goose grease. On a warm evening, you could smell Bernard before you saw him.

'A tiny bird tells me you're short of an act,' Bernard continued. 'I humbly offer my services. A little Lear, perhaps? A morsel of Macbeth? Or would you favour comedy? In the words of the Bard, "I am fresh of spirit and resolved to meet all perils very constantly".'

'I appreciate the offer,' Tansie said, 'I'm just not sure the Palace punters are quite ready for your level of sophistication.'

'One is always ready for the Bard,' Bernard said, affronted.

'I've thought of something,' Minnie said. 'Leave it with me.'

She ducked back down the corridor to the furthest dressing room. Five minutes later she was back.

'Sorted,' she told Tansie. 'Betty Gilbert. You hired her as a plate spinner, but the dog and monkey act could do a better job. She won't last two minutes before she's shouted off, but she can do a full turn on the tightrope. That's her trade. She'll need a little time to practise, but she's game.'

Tansie reached up, grabbed Minnie on both sides of her face, and pulled down her head, planting a smacker on her forehead. 'You, my girl, are a bloody lifesaver,' he said, a rare smile illuminating his face and revealing the glint of a gold tooth. He turned swiftly, and headed towards the stage, shouting random instructions at anyone he passed.

Minnie made her way back to Cora's dressing room. Just as she turned the door handle, Bobby appeared, panting hard. Minnie glanced at her pocket watch. Impressive.

'She ain't there,' Bobby said, catching his breath. 'Her ma ain't seen her since early today.'

'And she's no idea where Rose might have gone?'

He shook his head.

The boy deserved more than the measly ha'penny Tansie had offered. Minnie felt in her pocket and gave him a penny.

'That's from Mr Tansford,' she said. 'Know who he is?'

'Little fella. Big voice. Fancy suit.'

Minnie smiled. 'Exactly. And next time you see him, remember to say thank you. He likes to feel appreciated, and there might be more work he can send your way.'

'Thanks, miss,' Bobby said, turning to leave.

'Here,' she said, moving towards the table and finding the key amongst

Cora's make-up. She unlocked the drawer and gave the cake a last mournful pat before handing it to Bobby.

The boy's eyes widened, and he snatched the cake from her hand before cramming it into his mouth with hungry bites.

Minnie turned back to the mirror and tried not to think about Rose.

CHAPTER TWO

Charlie Moore was looking for someone.

Not any particular girl – he wasn't fussy – but someone half-way pretty would do. Here on the Strand it shouldn't take long. He wound his way through the crowds, sidestepping newly-arrived visitors to the city who stood in the middle of the pavement, gawping at posters for the Variety Palace and its various delights.

After a few minutes a hand rested gently on his arm and he heard a whispered invitation.

He looked at her. He'd had worse.

'How much?' Charlie asked.

'A bob?'

Charlie snorted. 'You must be joking, love.'

He reached into his pocket, drawing out a handful of coins, carefully keeping the rest of his money out of view.

'Look,' he showed her, 'I ain't got no more than fourpence.'

'All right,' she said. 'But we'll have to go down the Arches. I ain't walking halfway across London for a measly fourpence.'

Charlie baulked. The Adelphi Arches were a network of tunnels facing onto the Thames. Before the Embankment Gardens had opened, they had made an impressive sight from the river, huge arches topped by the houses of Adelphi Terrace. Since the opening of the Gardens, they were less visible but still impressive from a distance.

Close up was a different story. Anyone with sense kept well away from the Arches.

But she was only fourpence.

The woman led Charlie down Villiers Street, then through a maze of back lanes. Charlie kept his hands firmly in his pockets, holding tight onto his money and gripping the life-preserver he carried at all times.

They took a final turn, and the Arches opened up in front of them. It had been a while since the Thames had flooded, but the stink of raw sewage was still evident. The woman grabbed hold of Charlie's hand and moved forward relentlessly. Heading deeper into the darkness, they passed alcoves and passages housing horses, cows, and wretched humans. Charlie jumped, as what looked like a pile of rags suddenly moved and cursed him. In the darkness, the floor seemed to writhe beneath his feet with the scurrying of rats. He wanted to turn back, but was unsure of the way out, terrified at the thought of getting lost. And the woman had a surprisingly strong grip.

'Where are we going?' Charlie whispered.

'Not much further, love. I've got a little spot just over here. And a candle or two, so we can see what we're about.'

As they moved forward, Charlie stroked the curve of the life-preserver in his pocket.

Finally, they reached their destination. An archway indistinguishable from all the others, a mound of cloths in the corner that Charlie guessed was the woman's bed.

'Here we are, love,' she said, giggling. 'Home, sweet home.'

Feeling his way, Charlie bumped into a bulky object that appeared to be hanging from the ceiling. It swung slowly, suggesting something heavy.

'What the hell is that?' he said. 'Here, light those candles you said you had.'

'Hang on a sec,' she murmured. 'Just gotta find me scratchers.'

The match flared, and the sulphurous smell briefly cut through the odour of sewage and decay. She turned, sheltering the candle with her hand.

'Now, love,' she said, 'what was it you were saying?'

Charlie's eyes lifted to the object slowly swinging from the ceiling.

It was a woman. Her features were distorted. Her tongue, swollen and purple, protruded between her lips. She looked young. It was difficult to make out many more details in the half-light.

But on her feet were a pair of cream silk shoes, embroidered with tiny red roses.

CHAPTER THREE

Albert Easterbrook stood at his drawing-room window, looking down at the two women standing on the narrow path leading to his front door. One looked to be of middle age, short and a little stout. She was dressed in full mourning, although she had removed her gloves to fiddle with the crêpe edging on her collar.

Fiendish stuff, crêpe, Albert thought. As if the loss of a loved one weren't enough.

Even from this distance, he could see that the woman's hands were red and raw-looking. The other woman was much younger, taller, dark-haired, also in mourning.

'They're still there, Mrs Byrne,' he said to his housekeeper as she entered the room with extra coals. 'Should I go down and speak to them?'

Mrs Byrne tutted. 'And what kind of impression will that give them,' she said, 'a gentleman opening his own door?'

She joined Albert by the window, leaning forward and parting the net curtains a fraction. Albert saw the older woman approach the front door. She squinted at the brass plaque above the knocker, then licked her thumb, wet the brass, and lightly polished it with her sleeve.

'Well, of all the cheek,' Mrs Byrne said. 'As if I didn't have Mary do that only yesterday.'

'Finger marks, Mrs Byrne. Easily done,' said Albert. 'Maybe that's why they're here. A domestic position.'

Mrs Byrne shot him a withering glance.

'You know why they're here, Mr Easterbrook. It says so, clear as day, on that brass plaque that isn't good enough for madam down there. "Albert Easterbrook. Private Detective". They want your help.'

'Well, I wish they'd hurry up.'

The younger woman glanced up and saw Albert and Mrs Byrne at the window. She nudged her companion in the small of her back, said something and pushed her toward the front door. Within moments there were two sharp raps, a little louder than necessary. Nerves, Albert thought.

Mrs Byrne bustled out of the room and returned shortly.

'Mrs Ida Watkins,' she sniffed, clearly not yet having forgiven the impromptu brass polishing, 'and Miss Minnie Ward.'

Face-to-face, Albert could see that the elder woman's mourning dress, a thin bombazine, was worn shiny at the elbows. Not her first loss. She pushed up the black veil on her bonnet; her features were pinched and fell into hard lines. Albert glanced at her hands and noted the wedding ring that cut into her flesh, the finger grown fat around it. Mrs Ida Watkins. She followed his gaze and buried her hands in the folds of her skirt.

The younger woman, Minnie Ward, had an open, expressive face, with a curious kind of asymmetry that held her back from beauty, the mouth a little full, the eyes small and dark. At her throat, she wore a mourning brooch of jet.

Albert offered the two women the couch, sitting opposite them on an exceptionally uncomfortable chair he had been meaning to dispose of for some time. Ida perched on the edge of the seat and distractedly scratched at the crêpe trimming her sleeves.

'How may I help?' Albert asked.

Ida narrowed her eyes and looked at him sceptically. Albert was used to a confused reaction when people first met him. His voice betrayed his upper-class background, but he had the build of a pugilist, tall and broad-chested, with a boxer's flattened nose and heavy hands.

'Are you sure you're Mr Easterbrook?' Ida asked. 'You don't look nothing like your picture,' and she turned to Minnie, who withdrew a dog-eared copy of *The Illustrated London News* from her bag, opened to page five with the ridiculous pencil drawing of Albert sporting a top hat and monocle.

He winced. 'An act of the illustrator's imagination,' he said. 'I don't even possess a monocle, and it has been so long since I wore a top hat, I fear the moths may have made it their home. But I am, indeed, Albert Easterbrook.'

Ida glanced nervously around the room, her eyes lighting on a copy of *The Times* on a side table by Albert's chair. The front page carried a large image of Lionel Winter, a wealthy local businessman, who had narrowly escaped being trampled by a runaway horse and carriage the day before.

'A quiet week for news,' Albert said, following her gaze.

Ida sniffed. 'Not all news gets in the papers does it? My Rose ain't on the front page.'

'Rose?' Albert asked.

'My daughter.' She paused, breathing deeply. 'She was found on Saturday night. Hanged under the Adelphi Arches.'

'I am so sorry for your loss,' Albert said, the platitude failing to convey his genuine sympathy. Minnie shot him a look.

'And Rose was your – sister?' he asked Minnie.

'No. A close friend.'

'The police are saying Rose's death was suicide,' Ida said, reaching in her pocket for a handkerchief. 'But I know my girl, Mr Easterbrook. She didn't kill herself. And now I can't have her buried in consecrated ground. If it weren't suicide, I could have her moved.'

She turned away. Albert waited quietly.

'Could you tell me a little about her?' Albert asked eventually, leaning forward in his chair. 'Her age? Was she married? Children?'

Ida looked at Minnie. 'She was a few years younger than you, weren't she, Min? 19, not married, although she was seeing a lad. Billy Walker. No children, thank God. Lived at home. Worked at the Variety Palace, tightrope walking and acrobatics.'

'Had there been any change in her recently?' he asked.

Ida looked at Minnie again.

'We've both been thinking about that,' Minnie said. 'She had been a bit quiet lately. But not enough to make her do away with her own life.'

'People can hide things,' Albert said carefully. 'Rose may have been unhappier than you realised.'

Ida shook her head. 'Like I said, I know my girl. She didn't kill herself.'

'What do you believe happened?'

Ida took a deep breath and then spoke in a rush. 'I think she was murdered, Mr Easterbrook. I mean, you can't accidentally hang yourself under the Adelphi Arches, can you? Someone did that to her, and then made it look like suicide.'

She looked at him defiantly, as if waiting for him to laugh, or tell her she was mad. She even moved further forward in her seat, ready to leave.

But Albert did not laugh. 'Do you suspect anyone?' he asked.

Ida shook her head. 'No one. But there were some odd things the police found.'

Again, she looked at Minnie.

'There were marks on her wrists and her ankles,' Minnie said, fingering the mourning brooch at her neck. 'Like she'd been tied very tight with a rope.'

'Did the police offer an explanation for these marks?'

'They said it was part of her work,' Ida said. 'You know how it is these days, every hall's trying to come up with some new turn no one's seen before. The police reckon she were working on something like that. But I worked in the halls myself, years ago,' she said, raising her voice and leaning forward. 'You wouldn't think it to look at me now, but I was once a tumbling girl, just like Rosie. And I know there weren't nothing you could do that would leave marks like that. People pay good money to see beautiful girls, not cuts and bruises.'

'You said she had a sweetheart,' Albert said. 'Might he have hurt her?'

'I think Billy hit her once or twice,' Ida said. 'When she was found, I went straight round to Billy's, but he swore up and down he'd never laid a finger on her.'

'Which is a lie,' Minnie said. 'I saw the bruises. Billy's a doorman at the

Palace. He's handy with his fists. Can't always distinguish between those who deserve it and those who don't.'

'Could he have done this?' Albert asked.

The two women looked at each other.

'Maybe,' Minnie said. 'But the bruises weren't the only thing.'

She nodded at Ida, who removed a small gold ball from her bag and passed it to Albert.

It was delicate, no more than half an inch in diameter, and heavily engraved. A golden link was inserted, as if to wear the piece on a watch chain or from a bracelet. Despite its delicacy, Albert felt the weight of the piece as he turned it over in his hand. He looked up at Ida.

'We found it in her belongings,' Ida said. 'Some gimcrack I thought it was. But my neighbour works in Hatton Garden and he reckons it's gold. Now, why would she have a piece of gold with all that fancy work?'

'Another sweetheart? An admirer from the music hall?'

Ida looked away. Minnie reached across and took her hand.

'There was somebody else,' Minnie said slowly. 'She never said who. But he had money. Bought her a pair of beautiful shoes that cost more than a month's wages.'

Albert turned the gold ball in his hand, and then held it close to his eye, rotating it slowly. He lowered the piece.

'I'm happy to take the case, Mrs Watkins,' he said, reaching for a slip of paper on the table beside him, and writing down his terms. A quarter of what he would normally charge, but Ida was not to know that.

He passed the paper to her. She looked at the figure and nodded her agreement before handing it to Minnie. Minnie shot him a penetrating glance but said nothing.

'Mrs Watkins, would you mind very much if I kept this item for a few days?' he said, holding the golden ball in the palm of his hand. 'The markings on it are very distinctive and I may be able to discover more about its origins.'

Ida nodded her assent.

'And could you give me a description of Rose?' Albert asked.

'We can do better than that,' Minnie said, burrowing in her bag and retrieving a small portrait photograph which she handed to Albert. 'All the girls have them now, in the halls. For publicity.'

He looked at the image. Rose was gazing off to one side of the camera, her hair up, with a few carefully trained curls brushing her forehead. An earring dangled from her left ear, and a decorative fan was just visible, holding up her hair at the back. The image was carefully contrived, an illusion of sophistication.

'She looks young,' Albert said.

'She was,' Ida replied. 'And now she'll never get any older.'

A silence descended on the room, the only noise the ticking of the clock on the mantelpiece and the logs stirring in the fire.

'How does this work, then?' Minnie asked briskly after a moment. 'Do you tell Ida when you've found something? Or do we call on you again?'

'I shall keep you updated on my progress. Perhaps you might call again next week?'

Ida nodded, and Albert rang for Mrs Byrne to see the two women out of the house. She appeared with surprising speed, and Albert suspected she had been listening at the door again. Her manner towards Ida had changed. Albert noticed her giving the other woman the gentlest pat on her arm as she led her out of the room.

Albert went to the window and watched the two women disappear from view before removing the golden trinket from his pocket. A Stanhope, unless he was much mistaken. He raised it again to his eye and focused on a tiny hole on the surface, barely bigger than a pinprick and easily missed. Neither of the women had noticed it, he was certain. Inside the hole was a miniscule lens. It magnified a photograph of a man who, for all the world, looked just like the image of Lionel Winter on the front page of *The Times*.

TOM BENN
Afterword

Crime novels are narratives generated and sustained by questions and transgressions. *What* is the crime? *Who* committed the crime? *How* was the crime committed? And *why*? Different books, eras, modes and subgenres centre a different question, and elect to answer all, some, or like Joan Lindsay's *Picnic at Hanging Rock*, dare to answer none definitively.

What then, are we left with, after some questions have been conditionally answered, and the transgressors brought to a legal, moral or cosmic reckoning?

Good crime fiction often keeps the land but redraws the map to better welcome and trade with its neighbours. It is suspicious of borders, especially its own. It crosses them to comfort the disturbed and disturb the comfortable. It might interlope, interrogate, cross-pollinate, provide catharsis, excite outrage and dissent. And when it starts to over-rely on a trope, it won't be long before said trope is warped by others to reveal something true again, about itself and us. Crime fiction demands this flexible, sceptical framework for its own increasingly rude health. The eleven writers in this third MA Crime Fiction Anthology understand this. Irrespective of subject, setting, theme or prose style, each uses the multitudes of the crime genre to embrace and reflect who we are and how we live now. Each understands and respects the genre, even as they dismantle its traditions.

'A lot of people worry about technique,' Walter Mosley, a respectful dismantler, says. '[But] craft doesn't make art. Craft just makes good sentences.'

Good crime fiction needs goods sentences, but Wise Walter is right. Good sentences can't be all we are left with. You might find that these crime writers do provide answers to crime fiction's perennial questions when you read their published novels. But they don't claim to have all the answers. Crime fiction is written to provoke the uncertainties. Critic Scott McCracken writes: 'More often than not, we read [crime fiction] for the uncertainties provoked by the mystery rather than the security given by the solution.'

Over the two-year course, we tutors provide students with frustratingly few answers or solutions, and no doubt teach them little other than craft; to worry about technique. Yet here, over the preceding pages, is the postmortem proof they have learned much. They are already asking new questions. Which leaves us, leaves them, and leaves the crime novel, with plenty.

Acknowledgements

This anthology comprises extracts from the novels written by the 2019 cohort of UEA's MA in Creative Writing: Crime Fiction. This anthology would not have been possible without the support of the UEA School of Literature, Drama and Creative Writing in partnership with Egg Box Publishing.

We would like to thank our course directors Henry Sutton and Laura Joyce, and tutors Tom Benn, Nathan Ashman, William Ryan and Julia Crouch for their insights, good advice and support. We would also like to thank both the 2017 and 2018 cohorts for making us part of the family of UEA MA Crime Writers.

Our course has been privileged to have masterclasses from exciting and inspirational crime authors. Many thanks to Arne Dahl, Mick Herron, Nicola Upson, Benjamin Black, Erin Kelly and Dreda Say Mitchell for sharing their thoughts and approaches to writing crime fiction – all of which were invaluable. Thank you also to Professor Mark Wilkinson and the staff at the Norfolk and Norwich University Hospital Mortuary for a fascinating insight into mortuary practice and how to commit the (almost) perfect murder. It was an unforgettable trip!

A huge thank you to Rachel Hore and Nathan Hamilton at the UEA Publishing Project for managing the anthology publication, Emily Benton for her excellent book design and Sarah Gooderson for her thorough proofreading. Thanks also to editors Antony Dunford, Karen Taylor and Natasha Hutcheson.

The acknowledgements for the 2019 Postmortem would not be complete without us expressing our appreciation to the various pubs and restaurants around Norwich, particularly the Sir Garnet. They have supported us with buckets of prosecco, wine, gin and beer, enabling the finer points of boiled owls, stalking, ghost dogs, Scottish burial mounds, rural crime, real crime, London crime, flaming skulls, Japanese crime, dead rhinos and medieval manuscripts to be debated.

We would also like to thank the funders who support the scholarships that support our crime fiction writers, in particular: The David Higham

Scholarship (Crime Fiction) and The Main Scholarship.

And finally, a thank you to all our families and friends for their patience and support throughout the course – you have all made this possible and we hope you enjoy the results.